CARMELLA CONDEMNED

by

Paul Blades

Cover art @Can Stock Photo, Inc/neotakezo

Dark Visions Publications

Previously published:

Vol. I	Maddy becomes a Ponygirl
Vol. II	The Training of a Ponygirl
Vol. III	Ponygirl Champion
Vol. IV	Ponygirl Summer
Vol. V	Ponygirl Love
Vol. VI	Ponygirl Season
Vol. VII	Ponygirl Season

Watch for publication of the other books in the Maddy Saga:

Vol. VIII	Ponygirl Pleasures
Vol. IX	Ponygirl Peril
Vol. X	Ponygirl's Choice

Other books by Paul Blades:

Klitzman's Isle
Klitzman's Empire
Klitzman's Paradise
Klitzman's Pawn Part One
Klitzman's Pawn Part Two
Slaver's Dozen- A Tale of Klitzman's Isle
The Taking of Cheryl Part One
The Taking of Cheryl Part Two: Slaver's Bait
Comfort Girl No. 4
Sacrifice to the Emerald God
The Blue Cantina: Anna's Surrender
The Warlord's Concubine, Books 1, 2 and 3
Dreams and Desires, Books 1 and 2

CHAPTER ONE

Jeb looked across the table at the dealer and pulled a long slug of scotch from his glass. He had been drinking steadily for about two hours. His mind was swimming and the dullness of his brain competed with the pounding of his pulse. Three jacks, two fours, a great hand for five-card draw. Not unbeatable, but good enough for most. His opponent, a white robed Arab smelling of dough, sat across from him with one of those inscrutable Middle Eastern smiles on his face. His wide lips spread in a slight upturn beneath the finely trimmed, black moustache. The sunglasses sat on his broad nose like a 'B' movie cliché. Twice he had been caught bluffing. Jeb had been the benefactor once, a sweet pot of upwards of twenty thousand. The other had been won by the Britisher, himself only showing a pair of sevens. That pot carried a lot of green too.

But the pot now loomed mountainous before Jeb, with perhaps $100,000 in it, the accumulation of the losses of four or five jet set players. Jeb had another fifteen in front of him, the dregs of his bankroll. Maybe there was another couple of hundred at the hotel, but this was real money here. None left home either, except what he might be able to raise on the boat and what was left of the business. This was the problem with making a score, easy come, easy go.

But so far, it wasn't go yet. Three jacks, two fours. A lot

more had been won with a lot less. Maybe this was the night.

Carmella, his girlfriend, was, as usual, dancing up a storm in the cabaret down the hall. She had a way with these Middle Eastern types. Knew how far to tease them. Her 22-year-old body was tight, curvaceous, lean. Their natural reticence around Western women, their lack of knowledge of what makes them tick, made them putty in her hands. She was a luscious piece. All curves and jiggles in the right places. And passionate. A dream. But not for them.

The last two years with Carmella had been fantastic. He had never thought that he could need someone so badly. Since they had met, everything had been falling into place. She was his good luck charm. And she was here tonight. A really big score and they could set up shop somewhere, anywhere. A little play on the market, a few investors, in six months to a year he could be driving one of those six figure sports cars, wearing his sunglasses indoors at night. Why should Mustapha here have all the fat of the land just because his tent happened to be sitting on a half billion barrels of oil?

Sweat crept down Jeb's forehead into his left eye. He blinked it away. It wouldn't do to let the Arab see him get rattled. It was the Arab's play.

He spoke to the dealer in a soft, honey dripped voice. The dealer looked over to Jeb. "Monsieur, the gentleman would like to know if you would care to up the stakes." They had been playing a $5,000.00 limit, three bet max. Was the Arab trying to bluff him out of the game?

"Why not?" he replied. "He's bluffing," Jeb thought.

A whisper again between the Arab and the dealer, "The gentleman would like to place a $25,000.00 bet, monsieur."

Jeb nervously and unconsciously fingered the small stack of chips before him. The Arab could definitely count. He only had $15,000. Christ, he could beat this bastard and $25,000.00 more would certainly be the icing on the cake. "May I put in my marker?" he asked the dealer.

A short conversation ensued between the dealer and the floor manager who had been standing by, murmurings, nods, shrugs of the shoulders. Then, "Monsieur will please sign the marker."

The dealer slid a short pad over to Jeb. The gamble of his life, that's what this was going to be. And with the casino's money. Why not go for broke? "Perhaps the gentleman will permit me to see his 25 and raise an additional 25?" Nods were exchanged between the dealer and the floor manager. The dealer then spoke in short, clipped tones to the 'gentleman' as they called him. The 'gentleman's' smiled broadened, the light glinted off of his sunglasses.

"Yes, yes!" he hissed. Jeb's stomach took a turn. "What if, what if," he thought. "What if he's got me beat. No, no," he answered himself. "Full house, Jacks over fours, draw poker, its good, a great hand. I've got the bastard. $150,000 just rolling down my driveway." Jeb signed the marker, filled in $35,000. "Let's do it," he snarled as he tossed the pad back over to the dealer. The dealer tore the marker off and placed it in the pile. The 'gentleman' pushed over a stack of chips to the pot.

There was a small crowd around the table, silent, drinking up the drama. This was the kind of wide open, wild play that made this country famous. It made it a draw for the high rolling set: thrills and chills. Jeb saw Carmella's face peer in from the crowd. Her eyes were bright with excitement, her face flushed with her exertions on the dance floor. Seeing Jeb and the Arab facing off over a pile of chips that would've done a buffalo proud, she pushed her way through and stood next to Jeb.

"Baby, you're my good luck charm. We're going to be doing it in style in just one minute," he told her.

Carmella looked anxiously at the pot, the lack of any chips in front of Jeb, the piece of paper on top of the pile. "You've bet everything," she stammered.

"Yes, and in a minute it's all going to be rolling downhill back to papa," Jeb returned, circling her waist with his left arm. Such a shapely waist, accentuated by the tightness of the glittering dress, short, halfway up the thigh, cut low and tight in the breasts, pushing them together and up and out. No wonder these sons of nomads and shepherds loved her. Carmella said nothing, just stared at Jeb and then the pile. She licked her lips nervously.

"Sir, I believe you have been called," the dealer spoke to Jeb. Jeb's heart flickered for just a moment. High Noon. He reached for his cards, which had laid face down before him. He flipped them over with a dramatic flair. The crowd took in its breath and then burst into applause. Yeah, they knew. Jacks over fours. Fat City. Carmella squeezed Jeb and squealed with delight.

Jeb looked over at the Arab. And as he did, his heart froze. The Arab was still smiling. In fact, he was grinning widely now. One by one he began to place his cards face up before him. The crowd hushed again. First a three. Then a queen, both spades. Another Queen, a diamond. The fourth card was a second three. He held the last card down before him. The tension was thick, Jeb felt his muscles constrict, the rush of the scotch and the easy victory were behind him now. It was one of those moments that rang clear as a bell in your life, something you could recall with absolute precision for the rest of your days, that you could and would live over and over. The Arab teased the crowd, glancing up and smiling, grinning. He then turned his gaze on Jeb and the delightful female at his side. He turned the card over.

A third queen!

A wave of nausea swept through Jeb. He couldn't believe it. The whole pile and thirty-five grand he didn't have. The crowd was going wild, applauding, cheering. A hand slapped Jeb's back. "Good show, man, tough luck," he heard a voice say. Carmella's grip around him loosened. His stomach was churning. He couldn't think, couldn't really react, as if a giant weight had begun to press down on his skull. The Arab raked in his pile. The marker, now more like a warrant, fell off of the pile and came to rest before the dealer. The dealer scooped it up and handed it to the manager. The manager stepped up to Jeb, "Monsieur, would you please come with me so that we can arrange the terms for payment of the marker?"

Jeb felt panic rise through his chest like a wave. "Of course, of course," he managed to mumble. He pushed himself away from the table. He had supped to his full here.

"I'll be there in a minute. Bathroom," he mumbled to the floor manager as he stepped away from the table.

The floor manager nodded curtly. "As you say, sir," he said, and watched as Jeb guided Carmella over to the bar.

"Wait here honey, I'll be right out."

"Jeb, what are you going to do? You've gambled away all of our money. How are you going to pay your marker?" Carmella's voice cracked with nervousness as she spoke. He eyes were wide, her face ashen. The color which had flushed her face from the dancing and excitement of the disco floor had fled.

"Just wait here, that's all. I'll take care of it. Don't worry, it's my problem."

"Jeb, it's my problem too. I thought we were going to have a nice vacation. Now it's ruined!"

"Take it easy, will you? If they see us fighting they'll get nervous. Let's play this out. Once we're out of here, I'll think of something. Just relax, o.k.?"

"O.k, o.k. Just hurry." Carmella looked up to the bartender. "Vodka, please, Absolut on the rocks with a twist." The bartender took in Carmella's tall, slender, tanned form, a form clearly visible in the tight, glittering dress. He smiled slightly "Certainly, madam." he replied.

As the bartender reached for the bottle of Absolut, Jeb headed for the men's room. Stepping inside, he made directly for a booth, past the smiling attendant. He shut the door and sat down on the toilet. Immediately, his head started swimming again. He felt tired. The combination of the scotch and the stress had played him out. "What am I going to do, what am I going to do?" he repeated to himself mentally. His thoughts ran in circles through his head like a whirlwind. He closed his eyes and saw before him the pile of cash from the pot being raked in by the chortling Arab. He saw his marker slip from the top, coming to rest before the dealer who, with a nod to the victorious Arab, picked it up and handed it to the floor manager. That marker was out there waiting for him. As he sat on the toilet he couldn't help think of the marker as a huge, looming net, waiting to be thrown over him as soon as he stepped from the bathroom.

His thoughts also ran to Carmella, sweet Carmella. Yesterday, they had swum together in the lagoon on the far side of the island. They had driven out in a rented convertible, laughing, relaxed and carefree, three weeks of vacation ahead of them. They made love after their swim, long and tenderly, naked, the sand clinging to their bodies. He could feel the warmth of Carmella's body, the tightness of her grip on his cock as it plunged into her, her legs crossed behind his back pulling him in closer, deeper inside. Her mouth fed on him hungrily, lustfully, while taking his discharge into her loins. Afterwards, they lay there in the sand and whispered to each other about the future, their hopes, their plans. Life had never been so good. And now it lay in ashes.

Still sitting, he tried to pull his thoughts together. "I've got my passport, Carmella's got hers. If we could just get out of here, we could go directly to the airport." A fifteen minute flight across the water, a whole other country. With a credit card or two they could be winging their way to the States, or at least Europe within a couple of hours. Once they got home, well, let them sue him. He might be able to raise the money in a few months with luck, certainly within a year, the way things had been going. His seemingly uncanny appreciation of the movements of the market, some shorts, some puts, some calls, a little luck, that was all he would need. He had done it, found the key, funded this once in a lifetime vacation. $35,000 was doable, but not right now, not sitting here in this rich man's crapper. He had to get away.

In the meantime, Carmella sat at the bar, tapping her foot nervously in the rung of her stool. Holding her drink tightly with her left hand, she busily swirled the ice with the swizzle stick in her right. Downing the rest of the vodka she nodded to the bartender for another. She couldn't decide if she were more pissed off or alarmed. Sure, she knew Jeb was a risk taker, a gambler of sorts. Sure, the money was his. He earned it; she had no claim on it. But to gamble away all of their plans together, that was a kind of theft. She had stood by him, had encouraged him, had held him in her arms when he was way out there on a limb, scared and needful. And he had just dumped everything in a trashcan. Full house or no full house, he had no right to do it. A small tear formed at the edge of her right eye. The bartender approached.

"I am sorry mademoiselle, the manager has instructed me that your credit is temporarily in question. Please understand."

A flash of anger whipped across Carmella's face. And now, humiliation. She would add this to the list to be laid at Jeb's door. From her left a deep male voice spoke out in Arabic. She looked over and saw a well dressed, dark complexioned man, around fifty, tall, with short clipped black hair and a neat, trim moustache. A small cluster of jewels sparkled briefly from a ring on his right pinky as he reached over to the bar to knock the ashes from his cigarette. He smiled at Carmella. A gentle smile, but mature, manly. "Excuse me, mademoiselle," he said. "I have taken the liberty of buying your next drink. I do not mean to offend, but you seemed to be somewhat distressed. I apologize if my small intrusion into your affairs is unwanted"

Carmella was used to men wanting to buy her drinks. Just tonight, if she had accepted half of the offers from the dainty, young Arab boys in the cabaret she would be laying there passed out with her dress up around her neck. Liquor is quicker, so they say, and these little rich boys seemed to believe that all they had to do was show her their bankroll and squirt a little booze into her and she would be on her knees doing a lip tango on their tools. Her mind was a little fuzzy even so. This thing with Jeb, the Absolut she had pretty much shot back, the dancing, the heat of the desert outside and now this handsome, sugar daddy type. Well, why not? She definitely needed the drink. And if Jeb didn't care enough about their relationship to risk losing everything, well, what was holding her back?

"Thank you Mr....." Carmella hesitated.

"Please call me Harry."

"Yes Harry, thank you, I think I will take that drink." The bartender had already poured it and was standing there before her smiling, grinning really. "Do all the people here smile all the time?" she asked herself.

"Actually my name is Harim Baroof, but Harim seems somewhat rustic and archaic, no?"

"No, not to me," Carmella replied, "but just the same, thank you for the drink."

"I cannot resist a damsel in distress. And such a beautiful one no less"

Here it comes, thought Carmella, the pickup lines, the hand on her knee, the greasy palm on her bare back, a vulgar whisper in her ear. But then, she sensed that Harry was somehow different. He carried himself so regally, standing about six feet tall, broad shoulders, his face smooth but with a short scar just below the right eye. If this were New York, she thought, well, who knows what could happen? But here, 6 or 7 thousand miles away from home, dead broke, and her boyfriend, fiancé really, just about to enter stage left, well, nothing could happen here. She wouldn't let it, couldn't even think about it.

"Well, not distress really, my fiancé has our cash and he's in the men's room. But thank you anyway."

"My pleasure mademoiselle, perhaps some day I can offer you a more extended hospitality. But for now, adieu." He nodded slightly and stepped away.

Carmella watched as Harry stepped back into the Casino

portion of the club. As he did, Jeb returned, passing Harry without looking up. She felt slightly ashamed of her wandering thoughts as she saw the disheveled, obviously worried Jeb step up to the bar. She downed a big gulp of her drink as Jeb slid onto the stool next to her. He pulled a small roll of cash from his pocket and threw two $100.00 bills on the bar. To the bartender he called for a Glennfiddich, a double, straight up, and his tab. He looked over at Carmella.

"Listen, I'm going to give these people the slip. This doesn't involve you. While I go downstairs to speak to the manager, I want you to leave here and go straight to the airport." Jeb was whispering, but with a note of panic in his voice. She had never seen him like this.

"But Jeb," she started, but held back as the bartender delivered the four fingers of scotch. The bartender scooped up the cash and walked away. "What about our stuff, our clothes? How can we just leave? What about the bill at the hotel?"

"Listen to me, Carmella, and listen good. I'm in deep shit." Jeb's voice was tense, pre-explosive. "I don't know what laws there are in this place, but I'll bet they don't take well to foreigners dropping bad paper on their gaming tables. And I don't intend to spend day one in any local jail wondering when my ambassador is going to arrive. And, I imagine that they'll want to detain you as a witness of some sorts. Do you want that? I mean for Christ's sakes, Carmella, this is real trouble."

Carmella held back her retort while the bartender delivered the change. Another of those insipid smiles. What hatred and ill feeling did they hide? "Do they detest us all so much?" Carmella wondered. After the bartender left, she let loose.

"Listen Jeb, I can't believe that you've done this. You've ruined everything. Did our relationship mean so little to you that you could just throw it away on a gambling table? And now you want me to leave all my things, my jewelry, my clothes, all the mementos of our trip, and flee the country like some kind of criminal? I just can't believe this is happening."

"Carmella," Jeb's voice was at the edge of hysteria. "I can't believe that you don't understand what's going on here. This isn't America. This isn't even a place where they have an elected government. We don't have any rights here. They chop off people's hands for stealing, even worse. Don't you think that if I can't pay these people will send me to prison, if I'm lucky? Do you want that on your head just because you were worried about your trinkets and souvenirs?" Jeb paused to look Carmella in the eyes. "I know I've fucked up. I'm sorry. If I could take it back I would. But I can't. I'll make it up to you somehow, I promise. And I'll pay the debt when I get the money, but right now I have no way to get it, not without calling in a lot of old favors. And I certainly wouldn't be able to do that from a jail cell or hanging from my thumbs in some dungeon."

Carmella watched Jeb's face as he talked. She could see the tears welling up in his eyes. She loved him. And she knew that deep down, he loved her. The last two years with Jeb she had been on a ride on a cloud. Her soul and her flesh craved him. He was about ten years older than her, turning the cusp from a boy to a man. Sometimes the boy still came out, like tonight. But she loved him. She would do whatever he wanted. To save him. To save their love.

"Okay, Jeb, I'll do what you want." Her hand lay on his arm. Their joined flesh tingled with electricity. "Just be careful, okay?"

Jeb let out a broad sigh of relief. “Carmella, I love you so much. I'm so sorry. Believe me, I'll make it up to you, I really will.”

Carmella looked tenderly at Jeb and caressed his face gently. She did love him. She reassured him, “It's okay, Jeb, it'll work out somehow.”

Jeb took a long pull at his drink, grimaced as the fiery scotch shot down his throat. “Here's what you do. I'm going to go into the office and lay down a line of bullshit. I don't know what else to do. I'll tell them that I need to call New York and have money wired over from the States. I want you to go directly to the airport. Use your credit card and buy a ticket for yourself to Cyprus leaving first thing in the morning. Buy another one from a different airline in your name again to Athens. Leave the Cyprus ticket in an envelope for me at the American Express office. You fly to Athens and book into the Alexandria Hotel. I'll be there as soon as I can get a transfer from Cyprus.”

“Jeb, how will you get out?”

“Don't worry, I have a little cash. All I need is to slip the casino security people and lay a little grease on one of the local monkeys and I'll be on my way.” He finished the Glenfiddich and stood. “Honey, I'm sorry for all this, I'll make it up to you as soon as we get back to the States.” Carmella reached out and put her arms around Jeb. They kissed, a long, deep, passionate kiss, a kiss of parting lovers. Jeb felt her warm, lithe body press firmly against his. Memories of their lovemaking flashed through his mind. Carmella felt this too, but also the love and caring that she needed from Jeb, the commitment to her, to them, to a future together.

Reluctantly, they drew their lips apart. Carmella, with

tears in her eyes now too, grabbed her purse from the bar and walked briskly towards the lobby of the casino. Her steps echoed loudly as her heels struck the marble floor. She could feel Jeb's eyes burning into her back. The hour was late. Two elegant and tipsy patrons were waiting at the door for a taxi as Carmella stepped down the front stairs. The desert air was hot, blasting hot, compared with the coolness of the casino. The heat made Carmella's mood more oppressive as she waited her turn. The laughter of the man and woman who waited with her was annoying, disconcerting. Sure, they could laugh, they weren't about to leave their possessions behind and high tail it out of the country. They hadn't just seen their vacation go down the tubes, sucked down by a trey of queens.

Finally, a cab arrived and the drunken couple was sped away into the night. Carmella dug into her purse for some cash while the doorman signaled to a car that was just pulling up to the taxi stand. Carmella stepped into the cab as the doorman opened the door. She always felt self-conscious stepping into a car while wearing her shorter skirts, especially here, where the average male had probably not seen good pair of legs outside of a magazine. She could feel the doorman's eyes molest her thighs as she leaned over to enter the car. She could not prevent her skirt from rising slightly, and then even further as she stepped up to get in. As she did, she felt just the slightest nudge on her thigh, behind her knee. Was it the doorman's hand, or was it her imagination? She turned and looked as the car began to move and could see him watching the cab speed away, the sickening, slavish grin, which so many of these men wore, on his face. Or was he smirking at her?

CHAPTER TWO

Carmella shook off the momentary surge of revulsion she felt at the thought that this greasy doorman had stolen a moment of intimate contact with her. She had always been proud of her ability to stand up to men and prevent unwanted contacts or even propositions. She had loved a few men, only boys, really. Her boyfriend from high school, a couple of one night stands in college, a man she had met through a friend. That, her first real affair, had lasted almost six months, long enough to put her off boys for good. And then Jeb. He loved her like a man, confident, but with passion and caring. And you could underline the word passion. Something about him had brought out the most in her sexually. She dreamed about making love to him, she loved to feel his body enter hers, loved to caress his manhood with her lips, to feel its mass and heat inside her mouth, to hear him moan with pleasure as she stroked him. It made her wet thinking about it.

"Airport!" she shouted out to the native behind the wheel. The car sped along the coast road, past the hotels and the fountains. As they passed her hotel, Carmella felt a pang of disappointment about the things she was leaving behind. The jewelry Jeb had given her, her mother's ring, the little doll she took with her everywhere she traveled. Suddenly, she made her decision. A couple of minutes wouldn't hurt, especially since the planes probably wouldn't be leaving until morning. It was now three a.m. and the earliest flight probably left at sunrise or so, three hours away. She could run upstairs, get her jewelry and some other things and run back out. No one would be the wiser if she didn't carry out her suitcase.

"Driver, stop here!" she called out. The driver forced the car to a crawl, pulled to the curb, and then made a broad u-turn in the middle of the street. Carmella was shoved back in her seat by the force of the turn and then sat back up to point the driver over to her hotel. He pulled in front and rushed out to open the door. "Wait here. I'll only be a few minutes," she told him.

Carmella walked briskly into the lobby of the hotel and went directly to the elevator. In her room she quickly scooped up her jewelry from her bag. There were no pockets on her skimpy little dress and the purse was too small. She did have a travel bag, no bigger than a large purse. Surely, no one would notice. As she piled the small handful of jewels and her small panda doll into the travel bag, she saw Jeb's suitcase on the chair next to the bed. I'll bet he's got some things in there I can rescue for him. She went over and opened the bag. Inside she found Jeb's Rolex, worth about $2,000 she thought. There was a ring, apparently an emerald, some money, about $1500, and a diamond tipped stickpin. She stuffed them inside the bag. It had only taken about four minutes, the ascent from the lobby, the frantic search of the room and now out. She flew to the door.

As she pulled it open, she stepped back and gasped. A man was standing there, a man in a well tailored, Western suit. Another man stood behind him. Both men were tall, with that gray look that cops have. "Cops. Oh shit," she thought.

"Mademoiselle, I hope I have not frightened you, but I must interrupt your travel plans I am afraid." That smile again. The taller of the men stepped forward, forcing Carmella back into the room. "Your driver downstairs has been paid off. I don't think you'll be going to the airport tonight." The second man laughed shortly.

Carmella stepped backwards to the edge of the bed. The door was now closed. She sensed danger. The bag on her shoulder dropped to the floor.

"I see you have gathered up some belongings, mademoiselle, shall we see what we have here?" The first man reached over to the bag and picked it up. He was slightly taller than the second man, dark skinned, with a small moustache, thin lipped, his features sharp and cold. The other man stood back slightly, his face darker yet, with a meanness in it, like he enjoyed his work, whatever that was. He was heavy set, almost pudgy. The first man gave Carmella a small push and she fell back onto the bed. "Please be seated, mademoiselle, I think this will take a little time."

"You can have whatever's there," Carmella started as she rose to a sitting position, "It's only a few things..."

Later, Carmella couldn't be sure if she heard the crack or felt the slap first. But it resounded off of her cheek and sent her sprawling on the bed. The man waited until the force of what had happened hit her. Tears had formed, she had begun to cry. She was pulled back to a sitting position by her hair and slapped again, this time on the other side. She was stunned, too stunned to react. Afraid too, the kind of fear that random and personal violence begets. The kind that puts your stomach and your heart both in your throat. Something

Carmella wasn't used to. Very few people are.

Carmella was then pulled close to the man's face, up off of the bed, his hands in her hair, pulling it, causing more pain. "You will kindly await any questions I have for you mademoiselle. You are not at a tea party you know." The fat man laughed again. Carmella was tossed back down on the bed. "Now sit there and be silent." This last was uttered coldly, without passion, but with authority. Carmella sat.

The big man had stepped away and she could hear, but not see, him place the chain on the lock at the door. Meanwhile, the thinner man rummaged through the travel bag, pulling out its contents. The small amount of clothes, a bra, some panties, tampons, all the miscellaneous junk was dumped on the floor, the jewelry was tossed onto the bed; the money, pulled out and placed in his pocket.

"This is your property, mademoiselle?"

"Yes, er, no." Carmella's façade of confidence faded as she fought back the tears. "Some of it is."

"You seem to be most confused. You know false information to a policeman is a very serious offense. You are already in trouble enough, no?"

"I, I don't know what trouble I'm in, I haven't done anything." Carmella's courage was returning. "And how do I know you're police officers. I want to see some kind of identification. I'm an American citizen."

The man laughed. Carmella didn't like it. It was a 'fuck you' laugh, the kind the spider made when the fly asked permission to go home for lunch. The room suddenly darkened as the heavy set man pulled the curtains shut. Not a good sign at all.

"I will ask the questions, little one. You will give answers. Do you understand?"

Carmella's hand went to her cheek. She nodded. She understood.

"This watch, it belongs to Mr. Hammel, yes?" Carmella nodded. "And this stickpin and the ring, they are his too?" Again a nod. "And these other jewels, they are yours?" Carmella squeaked out a 'yes', her voice betraying her fear.

"And you and Mr. Hammel are not married, no?" She shook her head no. "And you were going to the airport, no?"

Carmella's heart sank. How could they know? Of course, the taxi driver. "Yes, but I haven't done anything wrong. I was just going to check flights and Jeb needed money, he needed to contact the States. The American Express office..."

"Mademoiselle, you are lying," the tall man interrupted, his voice stern and cold. "You are under arrest. You will be charged with fraud upon the State, aiding a fugitive, theft of government property, lying to government agents, bribery and attempted flight. You will stand up now and turn your back to me."

Not an invitation, a command.

Tears began streaming down Carmella's face. The image of a grimy, pestilent, Arabian prison rose before her, Midnight Express with a vengeance. It was unbelievable, this couldn't be happening. Just an hour ago life had been full, vibrant, a celebration of happiness. Now, she was about to be whisked away to the Dark Hole of Calcutta, or its Middle Eastern equivalent. She hesitated briefly before rising. As a result, Thin Lips grabbed her by her arm and pulled her to her feet. His grip was vise-like, pressing into her arm, causing her to wince with pain. She stumbled on her high heels, felt herself spun around and pushed face down back onto the bed. A hand pushed at the back of her head, filling her mouth and nose with the bedclothes, while other hands pulled her arms together behind her. In an instant her wrists were cuffed, the unmistakable click of the locks signaling to Carmella her powerlessness, her imprisonment.

She felt the pressure lift off of her head as the hand was withdrawn. Her skirt had ridden up to her hips in the struggle exposing her panties and the tops of her stockings. Jeb disliked pantyhose. He said that it cut down on their spontaneity. He liked to make love or caress her in public or semi public places. Often, in the car, in elevators, in offices or waiting rooms, whenever there was a moment or two when no one was watching. He would reach below her dress and caress her thighs or between them, kissing her deeply, getting her ready for physical love. And then, later, he would reap the rewards of her passion that had smoldered as a result of his touch. And so, it was a view of panties, a garter belt, stockings, and three or four inches of tanned thigh, which presented itself to the view of her assailants.

As Carmella regained her breath she was raised up off of the bed, her skirt still up above her waist. The men eyed her eagerly. Her face was still wet with tears, but the cold terror of the moment dried them at their source. The idea slowly worked into Carmella's mind that there was still a way out of this. Distasteful, yes. Unpleasant, even disgusting, taking into account the leers of the two men standing before her, but not undoable. Perhaps, yes, perhaps. No one would ever know, and she would be free.

“Please, please let me go,” Carmella managed to squeak out. The men laughed. The thin one, who was holding her left arm with one hand, pulled the hem of her dress higher above her left hip with the other.

“Oh, this would be such a shame mademoiselle, an offense to our honor. We are sworn to uphold the law and you have dishonored us with a bribe and sought to evade justice. These are serious offenses."

The fat man placed his hand on the elastic of her panties, sliding a fat finger inside, running it across her stomach. She tensed at the touch, her stomach muscles jumping back, a cold fear rising in her chest. She looked him in the eyes. He wanted her, yes, they both did. It would work, it had to.

"I'll do anything you want. I'll, I'll..." her voice faltered, "...I'll give you pleasure, sleep with you, whatever you want, just please, please let me go. I'll give you everything, I won't tell anyone, just please, please, don't send me to jail, please." Carmella's voice was frantic. She had intended confidence, bargaining from a position of strength, the strength that her sexuality and desirability gave her. But she was the one handcuffed; she was the one with someone else's hand in her underwear.

The fat man nodded at the thin one and Carmella felt the ground shift beneath her feet. It was going to happen. The fat man grabbed her by the hair and pulled her over to the center of the room. "Kneel!" he commanded, and Carmella lowered herself to her knees. Her dress was still at her waist, and the fat man pulled it higher, up past her breasts, over her head and off of her body. Since her hands were still joined behind her, the dress bunched down along her arms. The fat man knelt down on one knee before Carmella, grabbing her face with both his hands. He brought his face close to hers. She could smell his sour breath, feel the roughness of his hands. She shuddered as he placed his lips on hers, his tongue thrusting into her mouth. Grimacing, she barely resisted barring him entry. Her hands writhed behind her; her breasts were crushed against her chest by his bulk.

Although her eyes were shut, she could sense the thin

man as he drifted around her. She knew the sexual tension she was creating for him, just as she knew the sexual passion arising in the fat man who now possessed her lips. The fat man's tongue pressed deeper into her mouth, exploring, demanding, as he now passed his left hand around the back of her neck and dropped the other to her breasts. His fat hand squeezed inside the cup of her bra, near to bursting it, as he slipped her left breast free and then the right. He rolled her nipples between his thumb and forefingers, first gently, then harshly. Carmella at first tried to ignore the pain, frowning, twisting, pulling back from the fat man, ever so slightly. His left hand grabbed the back of her neck firmly, forcing her forward, keeping her in place. A moan grew slowly in her chest as the pressure on her breast became tighter, harsher. The moan grew into a whimper, then to a cry, a cry stifled by the press of the fat man's mouth upon hers.

Suddenly, her mouth was free. At the same moment, her breast was released. Carmella tried to catch her breath, recover. Things were moving too fast. She thought she would be in control, making the rules. She had what they desired, her breasts, her mouth, the flesh between her thighs. But was she bartering for her freedom, or were they just taking what they wanted? The fat man stood before her, his cock hard, pressing out from his pants. He rubbed his hand along its length, his other hand entwined in her hair. He spoke a few words in Arabic to the thin man and laughed. The thin man was sitting at the couch at the other end of the suite, bent over the coffee table, telephone to his ear. He looked over his shoulder and spat back a phrase or two, smiling, leering at the girl. Carmella tried to speak.

"Please let me up. Release my hands, I'll do what you

want. Just promise to let me go after, please." The fat man jerked her hair painfully, pulling her head backwards. With his finger across his lips he signaled her to be quiet. Another greasy smile. Carmella trembled in spite of herself.

The fat man drew open his fly with his left hand while he held the girl's head still with his right. His cock fell free, red and hard, fat and greasy. Gently, he slapped Carmella's face with his right hand, whispering, his voice now smooth, almost caressing. He slid his index and pointer fingers along her cheek, down along her chin and then across her lips. He then pressed them firmly between them, forcing them open, pushing past her teeth, pushing her tongue backwards into her mouth. Carmella gagged, whimpering in spite of herself. The man leaned over, his face next to hers, whispering, insisting, demanding, not in English, but in Arabic. His meaning was clear though, and Carmella closed her lips around his fingers. Her eyes were fixed on his. She wanted to look away, but couldn't. Just as one would be fixated at a bug, a snake, a beast, her gaze was fixed on the fat man. His insisting voice continued as he now moved his fingers back and forth between her lips. He pressed her face forward with his other hand, holding on to her hair behind her head.

Carmella's heart was pounding. She knew what was coming. She knew that the thin man would be watching, measuring her, awaiting his turn. She also knew, or, rather, hoped, that her freedom depended on her cooperation, her willingness, the pleasure she could now give. But, it seemed that the giving of pleasure here was secondary. This man wanted to dominate her, humiliate her, shame her. He was using her in a way she had only imagined. Sure, Jeb had used her body with freedom, and she had given it willingly. But Jeb had not taken her without showing that he appreciated her gift of herself to him, that he was possessing something precious, fragile, given with love. This man was looking for something else, something Carmella couldn't quite define, but it surely involved using her meanly, painfully, degrading her.

Carmella felt her head pulled backwards. Her knees spread wider to keep her balance as the fingers in her mouth pushed her back and the other hand pulled her down. The fat man straddled her body, his cock rubbing against her breasts, which swung gently together, her bra pushing them out and up, as it lay bunched beneath them. She felt herself falling, and glanced over to the thin man, now on the telephone, his back to them. The fat man's hand was now holding her neck as he guided her backwards, her back arching over her arms joined behind her. She tried to pull her legs from under her, but the fat man pushed her torso down, pinning them underneath. He knelt over her, his fingers pushing against the back of her throat. Leaning over, he first took one nipple in his mouth, then the other. Sucking hard, biting, crushing each breast in his hand, he placed his full weight upon the girl. Her thigh muscles strained, her face obscured by the fat man's hand, she tried to cry out in pain, but was stifled, the two fat fingers muffling the sound.

Slowly, the fat man slid his body upwards, towards her face, his cock stabbing at her chin. He spread his fingers within her mouth, distending her lips, the heel of his hand on her chin. The he slid his cock in between his fingers and into her mouth.

Carmella gasped as the bulk of his cock jammed against her tongue and the back of her throat. She struggled to breathe as her whole face was covered by his stomach and loins. His hands held her head still as he pulled back and forth, seeking the caress of her lips. Her legs were still pinned beneath her, her thighs flung widely open, her breasts crushed by the fat man's large buttocks. Slowly, he worked his cock back and forth, murmuring softly, almost singing. She could hear his breath as he labored towards his climax, a rhythmic bellows.

Although Carmella couldn't see the thin man, she could sense him watching her. She was fully exposed to him, her breasts heaving as she strained for breath, her legs spread. She felt suddenly ashamed, used, degraded, just as the fat man had intended. She was a vessel, a wanton one since she had brought this on herself. Whatever happened to her she deserved, had earned as the fruit of her sin, her lapse, her desire to use her sex as a type of legal tender. And while her mind flayed herself, at the same time she revolted, fought back, asserted her oneness, her inviolability, the wrongness of what was happening to her.

Her need to end this, to cut it short, to foster it along to its conclusion, overcame her fear, her feelings of violation and abuse. She sucked as best she could on the bar of iron that jammed against the back of her mouth. She flicked her tongue around its length, tried to move her head in rhythm to the fat man's thrusts. She could feel him rise, give in, adjust to her flow. His murmurings became a torrent as he began to move faster and faster. She could feel someone raising her body, pulling her legs free from beneath her. Hands caressed her thighs, soothing the muscles there. She felt the hands glide up her hips and then gently, smoothly, pull her panties down her thighs, over her knees and past her feet. Her legs were spread, a mouth fixing itself on her sex, biting, sucking, thrusting against her mound and the tip, the center of her pleasure. In spite of her fear, or maybe because of it, she felt the well known warmth flow first to her loins, then to her thighs, her belly and above.

The end came, finally, suddenly, in a gush of fluids, the wild throbbing of the fat man's joint, his cries of pleasure, his thrusts. At the same time the mouth left her sex and hands lifted her knees, pushing them up and apart. She felt a probing, an assault against the gates of her cunt, and then an entrance, a violation. As the fat man slowly caressed his now spent cock against her lips, the cock below began to rock her, pressing against her pleasure, filling her below. She was senseless now of her surroundings, conscious only of the pounding at her thighs, the press of flesh against her face. The fat man pulled off and her knees were pressed further upwards, against her breasts. Between her still stockinged legs, she could now see the thin man. He was grinning, his face red with exertion, sweat on his brow. She was wet, wet in spite of herself, against her wishes, against her volition. Disgusted, but at the same time fulfilled, she could not prevent the moan escaping her lips. She shuddered as a wave of pleasure washed over her. Her back arched, pushing against the weight atop her. As she did so, the man tensed and then exploded in a fit of passion, crying out and then collapsing.

The two lay in a heap, exhausted, he, his forces temporarily spent, she, laid low by a tide of agony and shame. The thin man pressed upon her, his face nestled in her neck. She could taste the fat man's sperm in her mouth. Her throat was dry, her legs ached. But at least it was over. She fought back additional tears.

The fat man was busy gathering together odds and ends throughout the room. Jeb's clothes were always first class and, although hardly a fit for the fat man, worth a good deal on the secondary market. He had broken into the courtesy cabinet and was downing a good part of a fifth of scotch. Packages of crackers and nuts lay opened across the floor and the bureau. It appeared that the fat man's appetites matched his size.

The thin man recovered his senses and lifted himself slowly off of Carmella. His cock slid out from her and she welcomed the restoration of that part of her body to herself. He zipped up his fly as he stood, remarking in Arabic to the fat man. Carmella rolled over, relieving the pressure on her hands, removing the two men from her sight as she turned towards the wall. Her dress still hung bunched at her wrists, her bra, pulled down below her breasts, across her chest. If she closed her eyes, thought of Jeb, Jeb waiting for her in Athens, their times together, their future, she could almost imagine this all away.

CHAPTER THREE

Jeb had met briefly with the casino security chief and manager. Ushered into the plush office in the basement of the casino, he had sweated it out as the manager apologized, spoke of routine procedures and asked how and when the balance of the marker would be paid. Jeb's head was clear now, as it had to be. Drinking sparkling water instead of scotch, he felt more in control. If he could just get clear of the casino. Carmella was already on her way to the airport, she would probably be gone by sunrise. He needed to keep these guys in play until then.

"Yes, I will call my banker immediately. I have a ready account of cash of about $150,000 in the Bank of New York. I guess it's about 4 p.m. there about now. We could just make it if you would let me use your telephone."

The manager bowed slightly with politeness. He was happy no doubt about the resolution of this matter. 5% of the pot belonged to the house and Jeb's portion was missing. Also, if Jeb welshed, the casino would be out the cash since it extended the credit. Not to mention the fact that welshers were bad for business. He handed Jeb the telephone. Jeb had to think fast.

He dialed 'O' and requested the international operator.

"Yes, in the United States," and he rattled off a string of numbers. A few moments, some clicking and clacking and then a ring. Two rings, three and then, "You have reached the home of Jeb and Carmella. We're not here right now...."

Jeb didn't wait for the message to end. "Phil Douglas, please, Private Banking." He paused for a few moments, giving a confident nod to the two sweating men before him. "Yes, Phil, how are you doing?.........Yes the vacation is great.........Carmella is fine. She's loving it here, the beaches, the night life, you know." Jeb laughed, "Oh, yes and some of that too." He covered the mouthpiece of the phone and whispered to the manager, "Nosey bastard. I hate this chit chat." And then again into the phone, "Yeah, yeah, yeah, Doug, but I've got to talk business.... Yes. I need some cash. Oh about $75,000.00 will do. Can we do it right away?.... Yeah.... Yeah.... Okay. Then do it as soon as you can.... Well that would be about 10 A.M. our time. Okay, yes, to the Royal Bank, you have the transmittal numbers there. And send my confirmation to the hotel. No, on second thought, to the casino here, the Oasis, yes, fax number is...." Jeb leaned over nodding to the manager. The manager jumped.

"Oh yes, yes, the number" and rattled off a string of digits which Jeb repeated dutifully into the phone. "Okay and you'd better liquidate another $50,000 tomorrow or the next day. Wait for a good rate. Okay.... Same to you. I'll see you when I get back. Goodbye."

Jeb rang off of the phone. The manager was smiling broadly. "I thank you sir, you have been most kind. We appreciate your prompt attention to this matter."

"No problem," Jeb replied. "I'm sorry that you'll have to wait until the morning. It seems the wire transfer room is backed up due to a computer glitch earlier today. But the money will be in early tomorrow. Before 10 A.M. he said. It could even be earlier."

"Yes, thank you, monsieur. And if you need a ride to your hotel now, I would be happy to..."

"Oh, no, I think I'll go try and get some of my money back upstairs. You have no objection to a credit of an additional $5,000.00?"

"Of course not, monsieur. I will arrange it."

Well, he had done it. If only he had known it would be so easy he would have had Carmella stay. But she was probably at the airport by now. He glanced at the clock, 3:25. The first flight to Athens was at about 5 A.M., if he recalled. The plane to Cyprus was a little bit later. An hour and a half, $5,000 to play with. He could just pull it off if he kept these fellows off balance.

After the appropriate nods and handshakes, Jeb was escorted back onto the playing floor. The crowd had thinned, but there was still considerable action. What to play? Blackjack? That would kill some time, but would the stakes last long enough? He couldn't take the chance of the manager seeing him cutting back on his bets. No poker. That would be sitting down with the lions again. Craps, that's it. He could let a few bets ride until he felt his luck coming on. A few passes with the dice. He might even get lucky.

He did get lucky. He watched a few passes before spreading $1,000 over the field. Cash flowed back like water. Fives, six the hard way, tens, nines, he brought back about $3,000.00. Then craps and the dice were his. He felt hot, felt like he was back on a roll. He earned another $2,000.00 and then faded. After a little over an hour, he was up about $1,500. 4:45, a good time to break off. He cashed in his chips, making sure he tipped heavily. Don't settle the marker, that's for tomorrow, he thought. Waiving to the security head, who was hovering by the main door, he stuffed the remaining money into his jacket pocket. Stepping out into the hot night, he signaled a taxi and got in. He named his hotel and the cab pulled off.

After a short drive, the cab pulled up to the hotel and Jeb stepped out. He tipped again handily and walked up the short set of stairs into the hotel lobby. For a moment he considered going upstairs. Carmella's things were there, a little more cash, his jewelry. No, not a moment to lose. He walked to the rear of the lobby, through the lounge and to the back door. Slipping out, he walked three or four blocks down the street until he saw what he was looking for, a taxi, cruising slowly. He waived it over. The driver stopped, apologizing, complaining, "Off duty, off duty." Probably among the few words of English he knew. But Jeb knew an international language.

A hundred dollars poorer, Jeb was speeding his way to the airport. Luckily, too, he had always insisted that he and Carmella carry duplicate passports. His now in his pocket, hers in her purse, they were able to abandon the ones held at the hotel desk. Now, if his luck could only hold. He glanced up at his hotel as the taxi passed it to get on the airport road. The hotel was mostly darkened, lights dim, here and there. He wasn't sure which one was his, the one lit third from the right, or the one next to it? Seven stories up, he couldn't tell.

* * * * * * * * * * * * * * *

The thin man watched as Jeb's taxi pulled away on the road to the airport. The hotel security man had called when Jeb left the Casino and he had been notified when the cab arrived. For a moment, he thought he would have to arrest Jeb as he got off the elevator to his room. A pity that, when things were going so well. The fat man had Carmella on his lap. His cock was jammed up inside her and he was lifting her up and down, impaling her. She had protested slightly when raised from the floor and thrown back on the bed. The thin man had had another turn with her there, slower this time, more pleasure for him. He had freed her hands and removed the dress and bra, her stockings and garter belt. She had cried out when her hands were joined again before her and he thought it prudent to tape her mouth shut. He had then entered her from behind, bent over the pillows. Now, as the fat man lifted her up and down, facing him, her legs over his massive thighs, he could hear her whimpers through the tape. He reached for the phone.

* * * * * * * * * * * * * * *

Jeb's taxi arrived at the airport at about 6:15. Why the airport was so far from the hotels was clear. Word could be gotten to the airport to stop a suspect much more quickly than any perpetrators could get there. Jeb could only hope that his fix was still good, that the casino manager hadn't checked on the call he had made, that the call hadn't been wiretapped, that no one had seen him slip out of the hotel, that the taxi driver would keep his mouth shut. With a handshake and a nod, he fled the taxi and streamed into the airport terminal. He walked quickly to the American Express office and, after hesitating for a moment, stepped in. A young, dark woman stood behind the desk. A diamond glittered in her left nostril. Pakistani perhaps, or Indian. No native woman would be seen like that, her face unobscured in public view. He approached the counter.

"Yes, I'm to pick up a ticket. The name is Jeb Hammel, my girl friend left it for me, Carmella Mitola."

"Oh, yes sir, here is your ticket. Straight to Athens. The 6:45 flight."

Jeb stood for a moment, confused. She was supposed to book it for Cyprus. Did something go wrong? And the ticket was supposed to be in her name. What happened? Did she get out?"

"Yes," he spoke to the attendant, "my girlfriend was supposed to catch an earlier flight, do you know if she got off okay."

"I am sorry sir. I came on duty only a half hour ago. I only know the note left by the prior clerk."

"Okay, I suppose she got off all right. We have to catch a boat you see and if she missed it, we'll have to make different arrangements." Cover your ass Jeb, he thought. Don't look nervous.

"Oh, yes sir. And if the young lady should call?"

"Tell her I'm on my way, that's all. Thank you. I see I have only a few moments to catch my plane. Goodbye."

Jeb strode quickly down the airport corridor. With no suitcase, he knew he would be suspicious. He had removed his tie and jacket in the cab, a tuxedo would seem out of place here. He watched as a young business type guy, obviously an American, carrying two bags of luggage, one large and one small, walked into the men's room. An idea.

Jeb came out another $500.00 poorer, but dressed casually and with a small suitcase. The businessman was sympathetic to a fellow being railroaded by a local business rival and good old Americanism helped a lot. So did the cash. Jeb walked confidently to the customs booth. The security at the airport was heavy and heaviest at the customs checkout. It seems that they were more concerned with who left than who came in. Jeb placed three crisp $100.00 bills inside his passport just before he got on line. The lack of an entrance visa on his duplicate passport would raise a question. But cash here spoke loudly and he had accomplished this particular sleight of hand before. He had instructed Carmella to do the same. As expected, the official glanced briefly at the passport, swept the cash into his pocket and stamped the passport loudly and with authority. A few short steps, the bag cleared without question, and he was through.

The plane taxied down the runway and Jeb sat back in his seat, his heart pounding. Even now, the plane could be called back. He would be in Athens in about an hour and forty minutes. Once over international waters, the plane would continue there regardless of instructions from the airport. He was minutes away.

The sun was up and shined through his window as the plane banked on its ascent. He could see the casino and the nearby hotels shrink away. He laughed. He had done it.

****

Carmella could hear the shower running as she lay on the bed. She had slept briefly after the last assault. Her hands were still joined before her, but the tape had been taken from her mouth. The thin man was on the couch on the telephone again. Room service had delivered some breakfast and the thin man was devouring his share. She had been on her knees servicing him when the food had arrived. She hadn't stopped to look, but she felt the eyes of the bellboy on her back, her exposed ass. The handcuffs rattled as she pulled the covers over her head with shame at the recollection. “Oh, God, please let them let me go now, please.”

A few moments later the fat man emerged from the shower. He toweled himself off and stepped into his clothes. The thin man stood and walked over to the bed.

“Mademoiselle, please get up.” As usual, his icy voice bespoke a command, not a request. Carmella pulled the covers back and slid her legs over the side of the bed. She stood before the thin man, her hands at her waist, joined together. Her head was bowed. The two men conferred briefly. Carmella could see the light flowing in the window, peaking through the blinds catching the dust, creating an impression of moonbeams into the room. She thought of Jeb. Where was he? They must have arrested him. If she were freed, would they let her help him, or would she have to leave the country? Could she help him? Dare she stay after what they had done to her?

The thin man pulled her over to the center of the room and unlocked the handcuffs. He lifted her dress from the floor and motioned her to put it on. She did so, quickly, without hesitation. Oh, were they really going to let her go?

As she dressed, the thin man walked into the living room area and sat at the coffee table as he had done before. The fat man was gathering his loot together. Carmella just stood there, waiting, her arms at her sides, not daring to look at the men. She needed to pee badly. Quietly she whispered, “Please, may I use the bathroom?” The fat man chuckled and jerked his head over in approval. She went in. He blocked the door open with his foot. She sat on the toilet and let the stream go.

“Oh please, a moment of privacy just to wash away the

filth these men put inside me," she thought. A shower, to wash away the saliva and sperm spilled on her, a mouthwash to wash away the taste of their cocks and their tongues, which had defiled her mouth. She could see herself in the floor length mirror across the wall of the bathroom. Her hair disheveled, her makeup all smeared, bags below her eyes, cheeks puffy from crying. Her loins ached as did her thighs. Her ass had been violated only by the fat man's fingers, and yet even there she felt injured, damaged. Her wrists were red from the handcuffs, and she rubbed them under the faucet. She washed her face and was able to wash away most of the makeup with soap and water. Bad for her skin, but the least of her worries. The fat man watched her intently, like she was some strange breed of animal mimicking human activity. Well to him perhaps she was just an animal. He certainly was to her. And if she had the chance, she would kill him without a moment's hesitation.

After she had dried her face, the fat man pulled her out of the bathroom. The thin man was waiting. The moment of truth. What was her fate? He smiled at her. "Please, may I go now?" she asked timidly. "Please?" She was afraid of bursting into tears.

The thin man stepped forwards to her, his hand grasping her chin, pulling her closer. Without a word, the fat man grabbed her arms from behind and joined them together with his handcuffs. Carmella felt her knees collapse beneath her as she moaned. "No, please, no, I've done all you asked, please, please." The fat man's arms supported her as she went limp. His arm circled her waist, her head was pulled back. Something, a ball, or more like a large round sponge was jammed in her mouth. Bitter, wet, pungent, like hashish, maybe opium, drugs anyway. A liquid oozed from it into her mouth as it was compressed. She struggled to expel it, shaking her head, pushing with her tongue, to no avail. Tape was again laid across her mouth. Her head began to swim. "What was this?" she thought. Stunned, she stood there as the men gathered their trophies. Suddenly, she felt herself pulled forwards, into the hall. Her feet were bare. Wearing only the dress, without underclothes, gagged, she felt naked and very exposed.

A couple was leaving the room across from hers, a European man and woman, thirtyish, dressed for jogging, startled by the scene before them. The fat man pulled a badge from his pocket and waived it at them, barking a command. Carmella's eyes pleaded with the couple. Quickly they moved away towards the elevator.

"Some bloody mess," the man muttered in an English accent as they moved away.

"Yes, yes," the thin man called to them, "a thief and a prostitute. She is arrested. Have a nice day."

They waited until the couple got onto the elevator and the door closed on them. Carmella was then pulled in the opposite direction. The freight elevator was at the other end of the hall. Passing a chambermaid's cart, they stopped as the thin man pulled a pillowcase from the bottom. Carmella could see the startled face of the chambermaid as it was pulled over her head. Again her knees buckled. Her helplessness struck her like a blow. Her worst fears short of death, short of disfigurement, were being realized. Dungeons, jails, rapes, pain, all these flashed before her.

She was dragged the rest of the way down the hall and onto the freight elevator. She could hear the rattling of dishes on a room service cart next to her and the breathing and physical presence of the busboy who stood behind it. She was startled when the elevator went up instead of down. What was going on?

The drugs in the sponge in her mouth were starting to take effect. Her thoughts were becoming confused, her mind dazed. She felt inertia in her arms and legs. If it were not for the fact of the two men holding her she would have certainly fallen. As the elevator pulled to a halt she couldn't help wonder how many women this bus boy had seen trundled into the freight elevator, a bag over her head, handcuffed. A few? Many? Was this a measure of the power of these two men that they could waltz her through the hotel without fear of retribution?

Pulled again by her arms, she accompanied the two men off of the elevator. A few steps, some small talk, a door opening. She was pushed across the threshold. After a brief discussion, her arms were freed, the pillowcase was removed and her dress was again pulled over her head. She saw herself in what must be the penthouse suite of the hotel: a sofa and several easy chairs in the main room, two doors into what appeared to be bedrooms, a bar and a kitchenette. She had only the time to glance quickly across the room before she was pulled to the center and forced to the floor. Her hands were bound anew behind her, this time with what felt to be a silken sash or rope. Her ankles were also crossed and tied, and then connected to her wrists behind her back. She felt herself pushed over on her side.

The fat man looked into her eyes. She looked back, her terror muted by the drugs. But the experience of the fat man's face inches from her own, leering, his breath hot, sour, would last and haunt her. Especially since it was the last thing she saw as the pillowcase was again draped over her head. This time it was secured by a cord around her neck. She could breath, but could see only a dim light through the cloth of the pillowcase. Hands rubbed her breasts, slid down her belly and grabbed her sex. Some words in Arabic, whether to her or to another she could not tell. A laugh, then footsteps, the door, then silence. She was alone.

CHAPTER FOUR

It was seemingly hours later that Carmella began to come back into consciousness. She had drifted in and out, back and forth, dreaming, floating. She knew her arms and legs ached, were cramped, but she didn't feel it. She also knew that she was hungry, but that too was something distant, something she knew more than felt. Her mouth was another question. She could feel the sponge inside, oozing more liquid and drugs each time she tried to dislodge it. It seemed that the liquids of her mouth were absorbed by the sponge, mixed with the drug base inside and then discharged back into her mouth. Each time she felt that she was coming out of it another blast from the sponge would take her under. But now, even the drugs in the sponge must be wearing off, she thought, because she could think, could begin to feel. And that wasn't all for the good.

Terror was the strongest emotion. What was going to happen to her? These men operated outside of the law, but seemed to be the law. But although they apparently cast fear wherever they went, they themselves were fearful when confronted by the English couple. Maybe there was some control over them. Maybe she just had to outlast them, stay alive, hang in there and she would make it. Certainly they couldn't kill her. Someone, Jeb, her father, her ambassador, someone would look for her, help her.

She strained at her bonds. Her wrists were joined firmly, not too tightly so as to cut off her circulation, but tight enough to prevent her slipping her hands free. The same with her ankles. She had to be careful as the more she struggled, the tighter it seemed that her bonds became. Her head was hot within the pillowcase and sweat dripped into her eyes. Her breath, trapped within the pillowcase, was stale. As she lay on the floor, her whole body felt dirty and disgusting. And again, she had to pee.

A noise at the door made Carmella jump. She could hear, but of course not see, two, maybe three people enter the room. She heard a woman's startled voice, not English. Hindi? Arabic? Carmella felt a momentary surge of hope. Maybe this was help. She could be freed, escape to the Embassy, anywhere. She whimpered in spite of herself. She rolled over to her back, ashamed, as her legs spread open, her breasts exposed. She tried to lift her head. Definitely two women. She could hear them whisper to each other. “Help, help” she tried to call out, her voice muffled by the tape across her lips, the sponge in her mouth and the pillowcase over her head. And then her hopes collapsed.

A man's voice, a heavily accented English, “Never mind that, just do your work.” The women quickly stepped away. Carmella began to sob. She felt her legs pulled apart, a hand on her thigh, on her sex. She tried to squirm away, but a hand held her leg tightly. A man's laugh. “Take it easy woman, just relax and enjoy yourself,” a thickly accented, harsh voice said. The man's thumb pressed inside her as his hand lay atop her lower belly. He rubbed her clitoris back and forth, which the discomfort of her retained water made excruciating. She knew that if he continued, she wouldn't be able to hold it in. She lay still and tried to concentrate. She heard noise at the door, carts rolling in. The hand left.

The man spoke again. “Here she is. Clean her up and feed her. This place has to be ready in an hour.” His footsteps fell away as small, soft hands gently closed her legs and pushed her to her side. Her ankles were freed. A soft feminine voice cooed at her, calming her. Her legs were gently extended, rubbed and massaged. Another set of hands joined in and she was gently lifted to her feet. She could not stand at first, but was steadied by a woman at either side of her. The pillowcase was removed from her head. She was guided across the room, through a threshold, and into a large, luxurious bedroom. A canopied bed stood in the center. Dark, heavy furniture lay against the walls. A bathroom was off to the left. The young women led Carmella into the white tiled room. She was lowered onto a toilet and she let the water flow.

As she peed, she watched the two dark skinned, Asian women who had helped her into the bathroom. The one was beginning to run a bath for her, the other standing by, holding her steady. Her hands were still bound behind her and the gag was still in her mouth. The activity of walking across the room had made her dizzy. The drug fog lingered at the corners of her mind. She allowed herself to be gently lifted off of the throne and led to the tub. Her hands were freed and she stepped in. The water was warm, soothing, she leaned back, closing her eyes, a shiver of self pity and shame running through her body. The gag was removed slowly, gently, and she nodded to the women with thanks. What was going on here was beyond her ability to think at the moment, but the surcease of pain and discomfort was welcome.

The two women quickly washed her hair and face. She

was then stood up and her body was soaped and rinsed. Special attention was paid to her loins and breasts. The women's fingers were supple yet strong as they worked their way across her body. She felt soothed by their competence, grateful for their silence. They were young, but somewhat older than Carmella, their relative age giving her some comfort. Yet, she was surprised at their lack of surprise. Was this some regular function of theirs? Could they be trusted to help her? Were they some sort of prisoners too? Why was this happening to her now, this almost ritual cleansing?

Carmella lost her opportunity to cross question the two women since, as she was stepping out of the tub with their assistance, the door to the bathroom opened and the thin man, the cop from before, stepped into the room. He barked an order to the women and they hustled her out into the bedroom. The fat man was there, sitting on the bed, eating from a tray. Beside him, also on the bed was a young, attractive Arabic woman, sitting crossed legged and glancing through a magazine. She looked up at Carmella, sneered and resumed her reading. She was dressed in native garb, with a flowing robe and sandals. There was a jewel through her nostril and her mouth was painted a bright red.

The thin man emerged from the bathroom, pulling up his fly, as the two Asian women began to dry Carmella. She stood there passively as the towel was rubbed against her skin. The women's touch was hurried now, almost frantic, as they strove to finish their chore. Suddenly the women were waived off by the thin man and fled the room. The door shut. The thin man approached Carmella and grabbed her still wet hair. He barked to the Arabic girl on the bed who looked up and nodded, barking back. The two men laughed and left the room, the fat man stopping, squeezing Carmella's breast and leering into her face before he walked away.

Watching the men leave, Carmella felt a well of resistance rise within her. What was going on here she didn't know, but she knew it would be no good for her. The Arab woman sat reading her magazine for a few moments while Carmella stood silently before her. Her breast burned from the fat man's touch. Her hair, still wet, but having been combed clear by the Asian maids, dripped water down her shoulders. Suddenly, the woman on the bed looked up and squawked at Carmella, pointing to the tray of food partially consumed on the bed. It was a large plate of couscous mixed with meat, lamb, most likely, a small bowl of some vegetables and a glass of water. Carmella's stomach, unfilled for God knows how long, rumbled and complained. She hadn't even realized that she was hungry, hungry and thirsty. Her head ached, she still felt woozy from the opiate she had been given, but her stomach was coming back to life. Survival, that was the most important thing.

Carmella dove into the food. She downed the glass of water and then stuffed her mouth full. The Arab girl watched her stonily, as if watching a camel chew its cud. Carmella ignored her and filled her belly. When she was finished, she looked up again at the Arab. She was reading her magazine again and Carmella took the opportunity to rise from the bed and return to the bathroom. She peed again and looked at herself in the mirror. No makeup, lines under her eyes, some black and blue spots beginning to show on her legs and arms. She felt suddenly tired. What if she just ran out of the door now? Why couldn't she just leave? Tired and scared, she peered out of the bathroom door. She could hear voices in the outer room. The cops? She would be beaten if she tried to escape. She just knew it. She closed the bathroom door and, sitting on the bathtub, she began to sob.

* * * * * * * * * * * * * * *

Jeb had arrived at the Alexandria Hotel at about noon. No word from or about Carmella. He was frantic. He was safe, but where was she? Where could she have gone? His calls to the airline had been fruitless, 'policy' forbidding them to reveal the names of passengers. He had called the answering machine at home in the States, no message there. There was no answer to her cell phone. What was left? He couldn't call Carmella's family or friends. That would just start them off panicking. Carmella's family generally didn't care for him and the feeling was likewise. But what to do?

It was now after 4 P.M. and still no word. Jeb decided that he had to call the Embassy. Something was definitely wrong. At least they could find out if she had been arrested. A chill ran through his body. Carmella, arrested, because of him.

* * * * * * * * * * * * * * *

Carmella had crawled to the corner of the bedroom and had fallen asleep. She dreamed about Jeb. He was falling away from her, calling back. She was stuck, unable to move, her feet encased in cement. Fire was growing around her. She waved frantically at Jeb, calling, crying out. The fire licked her thighs, her buttocks, burning, tormenting her. Suddenly she was awake. The Arab girl was standing over her. She held a leather switch in her right hand. She was prodding

Carmella with her foot, shouting an order at her. She had been whipping Carmella awake. Again the switch came down across Carmella's thighs, burning her.

Carmella leapt to her feet, crying, twisting away from what now was a rain of blows. She tried to grab the switch, but the Arab girl slapped her across the face, grabbed her arm and twisted it behind her. She felt herself propelled to the bed, her arm pulled up to her shoulder blade. Crying out in pain, Carmella begged the girl to stop hurting her. Four more blows fell across her tender rear cheeks. She was released. After giving her a moment to recover, the girl motioned Carmella to get up from the bed. Carmella obeyed at once, knowing that she didn't have the strength to fight this little powerhouse of a girl. Following the girl's instructions, Carmella got down on her knees, her legs apart, her hands behind her head. The girl examined her handiwork for a moment and then disappeared behind Carmella. Carmella waited anxiously. What was this? What was happening now?

The girl approached Carmella from behind. She felt a belt looped around her waist and joined behind her back. First her right hand, then her left was tied tightly to clamps on either side of the belt, slightly above the hip. Carmella, afraid to speak or beg, merely whimpered. The girl left again for a moment and then returned with a chair and a small bag from which she drew makeup and perfume. Placing the chair before Carmella, she sat in it and proceeded to powder and color Carmella's face and lips. Her eyes were shaded and lined, her lips and nipples painted red, her breasts, neck, armpits and inner thighs perfumed. Her hair was tied back to clear her face.

While being decorated by the Arab girl, Carmella allowed

her mind to wander, float free. Clearly something was up, but she didn't want to think about it. What more could be done to her she couldn't think. Survival, survival, that was all she could concentrate on. Having resolved to survive, she could drift freely in her mind, think of Jeb, the time they had together at the beach the day before, their life together back in the States, the laughter of a friend and lover. But, no, that laughter was from the next room, a woman's voice, high and shrill. A man's voice followed, and then another. Suddenly, music began to play. A party was starting, and she was the party girl.

Carmella was lifted to her feet and shaken from her reverie. The Arab girl shoved a gag into her mouth and she could taste the drug-laced potion within it. She panicked slightly, and attempted to pull her hands free from their confinement at her sides as the straps from the gag were pulled tightly behind her head. The Arab girl pulled her into the bathroom where she allowed Carmella to pee once more. She caught a glimpse of herself in the mirror, made up like a grade B whore, her brightly painted lips pulled back in a grimace by the gag, her cheeks heavily rouged, her eyes darkened. She was pulled out back into the bedroom, her mind beginning to swim from the drugs. Dragging Carmella over to the bed, the girl grabbed a ring set in the front of the belt around Carmella's waist, spun her around and pushed her down on her back. The girl spread Carmella's legs, and then, holding them apart, applied a lubricant to the furrow between her thighs, rubbing her fingers inside the opening, stopping only when she could slide them back and forth with ease. She then pushed Carmella's knees back towards her shoulders and repeated the process with the rear passage. Carmella was in a dream state, but the violation of her nether region by first one, then two and then three fingers brought her close to full awareness. She was being violated, it hurt, and then it didn't. She squirmed, moaning behind her gag. The Arab girl looked her in the eye and smiled.

While waiting, all decorated and greased like a sex toy, Carmella lay on the bed, the covers pulled back, the Arab girl gently stroking her breasts, her thighs, the entrance to her cunt. Carmella strained to resist the swelling feelings of physical pleasure. Her resistance, weakened by the effects of the drug, her mind needing release, needing to concentrate on something other than her terror, her shame at her violations, tugged at her will, “Let go, let go, don't fight,” it said.

Suddenly the door opened. The music became momentarily louder and then ebbed again to a dull pounding from the other room. Carmella drifted her glance over to the door. These weren't the cops. These were new guys, young, well dressed, swinger types. Nervously they tip toed into the room. The girl addressed them briefly in Arabic, cooing, pulling Carmella’s thighs apart. As the men stepped closer, she dipped her fingers into Carmella's pussy, waving the men to her side.

The men quickly overcame their reserve. The first one quickly stripped his clothes and jumped up onto the bed. He brought his gaze close to Carmella's face, slid his hands across her breasts, down her belly and around her sex. He smiled, murmured quietly and then, throwing his legs between hers, spread her lower lips and plunged his now erect prick deep into her lubricated gash. Carmella struggled, pulling at her arms, frantically tossing her head back and forth. The young man pounded away at her flesh, driving himself home deep into her sex. His lips stroked her face, her chin, her neck, while he grunted and moaned. She felt him stiffen, groaning loudly and then grab her hair tightly as he came within her. The second man insisted that Carmella be turned over on her stomach and then assaulted her rear end. The grease and preparation done by the Arab girl, not to mention the opiate, helped to ease the way for his invasion of this portal, but, pain, nonetheless coursed through Carmella's body as the delicate membranes were torn. She moaned and cried beneath her gag, her face forced down on the bed, her stomach elevated by a pillow, causing her ass to rise up, offering its delights to this sodomite.

The second man finished and the two men quickly dressed and left the room. Carmella lay crying, face down on the bed, the unimaginable now being real. She had only a moments respite, however, as the door opened again and another man entered. He rolled her to her back, spread her thighs and plunged inside.

Carmella lost track of how many men she serviced that night, and over the next two days. More than one she recognized as dancers from the casino, men whose temperature she had raised. More often the men were strangers, unknown or unrecognized by her. During breaks the Arab girl pulled her into the bathroom to wash her pussy and thighs, douching her vagina thoroughly as well as her rear, and then greasing them up again for the next assault. Her mouth was not spared, her hesitation at swallowing the first prick dangled before her face was cured by the crack of the young girl's whip. Otherwise, and except to drink and eat, such as that was, Carmella's mouth remained clamped tight about the opiate soaked gag.

Finally, on the third day, as dawn broke through the curtained windows, Carmella awoke to peace and quiet in the room. The music outside the room had stopped. The Arab girl was asleep at the foot of the bed. Carmella's sex and thighs ached, her violated mouth and rear were raw and sore. "Was it over, really over?" she thought. Surely it had to end sometime. She dozed off her hands still bound at her sides, too woozy and weak to get up and even try to slip out.

Later that day, shortly after noon, Carmella was awakened by the quiet and gentle whisper of some strange tongue. She jumped, startled, the terror of last three days and nights slamming back into her consciousness. Before her were the two Asian women from the first night. The Arab girl was gone. The women pulled Carmella gently into the bathroom and bathed her much as they had done before. Carmella ignored them, her mind rebelling against where she was, what had been done to her. Over three days, twenty, thirty, forty men, she couldn't remember. Who had gone when, what they had done, who had repeated themselves, all was a blur to her. She remembered the faces of her jailers more than once coming in to take their due. More than once she sensed the Arab girl servicing another at the same time that Carmella was busy on the bed. From time to time she had even been alone in the room. Other times she had awoken to see two or three men, sitting cross legged on the floor, waiting their turn, drinking, smoking, laughing. She had been fucked in the bed, on the floor, standing, squatting, bent over, every way the men could think of. Two at once or one at a time, every orifice had been ravaged and polluted. She didn't believe that she would ever again really be clean.

When the bath was done, she was returned to the bedroom where a tray of food awaited. Her dress was on the bed, her shoes below. She ate slowly, without caring, almost automatically, her mind accepting the urgings of the two women as commands. The belt had not been removed from her waist and she sat there, naked but for its slim covering, its straps loose at her sides.

When she finished eating, the Asian women left the room. As they exited, the thin cop walked into the bedroom. He smiled at Carmella, pulling her to her feet by the ring at the front of her belt.

"Well, my little sparrow," he said, "you have been a source of good fortune to me and my friend. We are very grateful that you agreed to cooperate with us. But now it is time to leave and return to the world. Are you ready to give up your new found profession?" He laughed at his joke. "But first, perhaps a little tidbit for good luck, eh?" He pushed Carmella back down on the bed, grabbing her wrists in his hand and lifting them above her head. She did not resist as he probed her loins, forcing his entry with his hand. When she was lubricated, he lay upon her, his clothes still on, his prick finding its target, pressing home. He took her, slowly rocking back and forth for his own pleasure. He pressed his tongue in her mouth, forcing his way, filling her.

When he was done, he pulled her to her feet and removed the belt from her waist. Carmella dressed silently as he watched, pulling her dress over her head, slipping her feet into her shoes. "Survive," she thought, "survive." She was getting out.

Down the service elevator, out the back, gagged and hooded as before, Carmella made her exit from the hotel. She didn't dare think what was in store for her, only glad that the days of imprisonment in the penthouse were over. "Live, live," she thought. The dope filled gag made her listless and tired and she was unable to keep track of the time in the car. It was really only fifteen minutes or so as the car sped across the small city to the police station and jail. The unmarked car sped quietly past the taxis and limousines carrying the tourists and wealthy to their rendezvous. There was no difference between their cars and the car in which Carmella was prisoner, other than their destination. Theirs were the casinos and restaurants, the playgrounds of the Emirate. Hers was its dungeons.

CHAPTER FIVE

Carmella barely noticed when the sleek, black car entered the garage beneath the jail and slid to a halt inside. She was pulled from the back seat by unknown arms as angry voices and the squeal of breaks echoed throughout the underground chamber. This six story monolith on the edge of the city was known locally as a place of no, or nearly no, return. The unfortunate who had no important friends or adequate money could only hope that Allah or his equivalent would have mercy. But if one of the high and esteemed wanted you in, you were in, and that was that. Coming and going underground gave the advantage of concealing from the nosy public just who was carried in the tinted glass cruisers and vans which went to and fro through the heavy steel overhead doors. No one had seen Carmella enter, and no one would see her go.

Once inside the building, Carmella was propelled down a hallway to an elevator. She rode up, she didn't know how many floors, and then down a long hallway. She felt the presence of two men with her, one on either side, each holding an arm as she was hurried along. Suddenly stopping, she heard voices, their meaning unknown, laughter, hands on her breasts, pinching her nipples, pulling her slightly up off of her feet onto her toes. She protested with a whimper. More laughter. Then there was a command, a sharp, important voice. The laughter stopped. Suddenly her hood was lifted, her gag removed. The lights were bright, too bright for her to do anything but close them and hold her head down. Her mouth was sore and dry, her arms tight behind her back. Whiteness was all she could see, the whiteness of the floors and walls, clean, sterile and cold.

She was flanked by the two goons who had held her prisoner for three days. She couldn't believe their gall. They had taken her to the police station. What they had done to her would justify the most severe criminal penalties in any civilized and most uncivilized places around the world. But here they were, dragging her into the local station house and charging her! But she knew also that right now silence was her very best friend. Anything could still happen here. Until she saw a lawyer, her ambassador, someone who could tell the outside world that she was here and alive, anything she said could precipitate her permanent disappearance. "Survive," she said to her self. "Survive."

After some bickering, and the filling out of some forms, Carmella was ushered inside the caged enclosure which served as the main desk. She was taken down a short hall into a room where she was photoed and printed. She was then taken to another room where she was stripped by a large battle-ax of a matron whose English seemed to be limited to "Off! Off!" Carmella slipped the now wrinkled and dirty dress over her head and let it drop to the floor. The matron then supervised a quick, cold water shower, stepping in to scrub Carmella in places where she was deemed to have been inadequately thorough. Her various bodily cavities were then explored, roughly, without malice, without pleasure; the same parts of her body defiled and degraded over the last three days. Somehow, this was different, businesslike. Carmella submitted meekly.

Her hair wet, Carmella toweled off and was given a drab, grey dress, which opened at the neck and covered her to her mid calf. For shoes she was given sandals. Carmella dressed, oddly grateful that this seemed to be a real prison and not a house of torture. She had created a vision of a huge stone structure with dungeons beneath the ground, racks and other torture devices, a hellhole of squalor. Instead, she seemed to be in a modern facility run coldly and efficiently.

Carmella was then led to a small desk behind which sat a small man in wire rimmed glasses. He motioned for her to sit and pulled out a file. She was a file already, good. The more records the better. "Name?" the man demanded. "Address? Nationality? Age? Marital status?" The normal questions. Carmella answered them automatically, quietly, almost whispering. This was the first time for three days she had actually been asked to speak. She had a name, a nationality. She had a place out there. A place where people would miss her, come get her, help her. Jeb? Where was Jeb? She started crying softly. The man looked up without expression. He nodded to the female attendant standing behind Carmella. As she felt her arm grasped and pulled upwards, Carmella panicked. What about her lawyer, a phone call, a letter, anything to get word out to get help? "Please, please," she said, "I need to see a lawyer. I need to call someone. I need help, please don't just send me away."

The man motioned the large female guard to stop. "You will have a lawyer assigned. You will be permitted to write a letter. This is not your United States, where the criminals have more rights than the police, but we are not in the dark ages either. You are to be held for examination by the magistrate. Before that you will be given the chance to speak with the lawyer. All will be done properly."

"But, what am I charged with? When will I see my lawyer? How long will I have to stay here? Can I make bail?" The questions poured out of Carmella in a torrent. She was still crying and her tears made her questions pathetic. The matron was dragging her away. Carmella struggled briefly. A crack echoed down the hallway as she realized she had been slapped across the face by the guard. The man spoke, "Silence is required at all times from prisoners, except when questioned. Please obey the rules. No exceptions for foreigners."

Carmella, in disbelief, was led down the hallway. Hooded again, her hands left free, she entered an elevator and was whisked upwards and then down. She couldn't tell what her floor was, or where in the building she was being taken to as she was dragged from the elevator and into the hall. Suddenly, after three turns, and at least seventy steps, she was stopped. A door opened with a loud clang. The hood was removed. She was thrust in. A cell. One bed, a sink, a toilet, a small roll of rough paper and a tiny bar of soap. No window, just the fluorescent light above, three walls around, and a set of steel bars in front. The cell was about ten by ten. The cell door slammed shut behind her.

****

Carmella was sentenced right after her trial, if you could call it that. She had known that she would be found guilty. Everything about her treatment after her arrest had confirmed that. No contact with the outside, other than one heavily censored letter to her parents, no talking with the other prisoners, no release from her cell other than a brief half hour per day of walking around a quite small prison yard. She had been provided with a lawyer, but her so-called lawyer had nothing good to say. She could sense his greasy lust for her on both occasions he had come to see her. His eyes wandered over her body, pausing at her mouth, her breasts, her legs. The prison garb was quite modest, a faded blue shirtwaist dress; buttoned down the front, hem below her knees. Unfortunately it was about a half size too small and obviously designed for the smaller breasted Asiatic women who made up most of the prison population. Carmella's breasts pushed the buttons to their extremes, her hips pulled the dress tight across her stomach and rear. Her attorney clearly enjoyed watching her approach silently on soft slippers, her head lowered as the guards had instructed her. Each time, halted just outside the glass walled visiting area, she submitted to the customary and thorough search of her person, the guard's hands patting down her sides, pushing up her breasts, splitting her legs to feel between her thighs. When she finally was able to look up, as she entered the conference area, she could see the appreciative grin on her lawyer's fat face.

The lawyer went over in detail with her the charges: bribery, prostitution, theft from the State, assault on a police officer, attempted escape, fornication with an unmarried male, and on and on. The list staggered her, but was not surprising. She knew that the men who had kidnapped her and held her for use as a sexual toy had profited by her numerous rapes and would not let her run off back to the real world and spread tales of their barbarism. She could only hope that, once the matter had been resolved, once she had confessed to whatever they wanted from her, she would be set free. Her confession would serve as a guarantee that any claims she made of abuse and rape would be instantly discredited.

Her lawyer led her to believe that this was the case. He had not told her what the penalty would be, but had reassured her that all would turn out well. "Oh, not to worry, mademoiselle, I have arranged everything," he said. "A minor penalty, that is all. I believe strongly. You will see." She would see. Well, that part at least was true. She signed the confession that her proffered to her.

The only trouble was that on the day of the trial, standing in the well of the court, the lawyer had leaned over and whispered to her, "I cannot say what will happen. They have changed the judge. All bets are off. I am sorry."

All bets are off? Her knees buckled as the guard led her to the special booth for defendants. Her attorney, taking his seat at the counsel's bench was now out of reach, out of communication with her. Her mind was spinning. Standing in the dock she watched and heard as the trial proceeded, in Arabic, of course, an interpreter translating what seemed to be every third or fourth word. "Affidavits. Bribery. Prostitution. Officers of the Law. Confession. Mercy." These were the words she could make out as the men bowed and nodded to each other. The judge was a large, imposing man with white whiskers, a flowing beard, right out the Arabian Nights; the prosecutor, a hawkish man, creased brow, with daggers in his eyes. Her own lawyer was obsequious, self effacing, bowing and scraping to save her from a fate she could not imagine.

The judge finally raised his right hand and the attorneys ceased their bickering. He shuffled the papers on the bench and looked down, for the first time, at Carmella. She put on her most forlorn look, knowing that an important moment seemed to have been reached. She had rehearsed her speech a hundred times, revised it, refined it, and then began all over again to find the exact words that would set her free. She looked the judge in the eye. There was that smile again.

But her moment to speak was not to be. The judge rolled his eyes, clasped his hands together and cried out in Arabic, a long wailing diatribe. He stared harshly down at Carmella, raised his eyes and hands to heaven, pounded the bench, appealed to the sparse audience in the courtroom, and generally engaged in every theatrical device Carmella had ever seen. It was a bravura performance, which spellbound her as the interpreter ejaculated various words and phrases at her: "Satan", "Allah the merciful and just", "law and order", "sacred trust", "imperialism" and then "guilty", "death", "mercy", "punishment", "service to the State", "seventeen years".

Seventeen years, was that her sentence? Was the case over? What was happening? Carmella felt faint as her lawyer turned to her, shrugging his shoulders in a helpless look. The judge and the prosecutor smiled and then looked down as they shuffled their papers. Carmella moved to speak. As she opened her mouth, the guard to her left grabbed her arm and pulled her towards the door behind the dock. Carmella stumbled and the guard caught her as she began to fall. Before she could cry out or react, she was through the door and dragged down the stairs that led to the cells below. Only then did she find her voice as she called out, "Wait, wait, please!" Her desperate cries echoed down the corridor. "Let me speak! I'm innocent! Please!"

Her voice merged with her sobs as the shock of what had just happened struck her. She had been found guilty of a crime and sentenced to seventeen years. Found guilty, but of what? Could she appeal? Was there parole? All these questions and more flashed through her mind as she was dragged, sniveling and weeping through the brightly lit corridor. On either side was a female guard dressed in flowing black chadors, bulky, muscle bound women, their faces covered in the Islamic style. Hers, of course, was uncovered as befitted a Westerner, an infidel, a whore.

Carmella was dragged past the entry to the jail from whence she had been brought to the courtroom, down a set of stairs, through a short, darkened corridor and into a large room. In the middle of the room was a block of cages, each one standing about three feet high and three feet across. Carmella cringed, trying to withdraw her arms from the steel like grasp of the two matrons. They pulled her into the room, twisting her arms behind her as she stamped her feet into the floor trying desperately to avoid whatever was her approaching fate.

As the bigger of the two matrons pulled Carmella's hair behind her head, the other let go a smack that literally rocked her teeth. She was struck again, this time from left to right. Carmella was dazed, stunned by the blows and slumped in the arms of her jailers. She was released, dumped on the floor. Carmella raised her head to protest when she saw the larger matron draw a long, thin stick from beneath her robes. A riding crop. Five blows landed across Carmella's back, her legs, and her arms as she raised them to ward off the blows. They stung fiercely, even through the thickness of her tailored jacket and skirt she had been allowed to wear. The message was clear. Obey.

The matron's shrill voice screamed a command in Arabic that tore a rent in Carmella's meager courage to resist. Carmella was sobbing, wailing even, too hard to breathe or to speak. She did not understand the words, but the meaning was clear as the matron emphasized her orders with unmistakable gestures. Carmella rose quickly to her feet and began to undress.

Twice while awaiting trial she had been beaten by the matrons; once, on her first day, just to teach her who was boss. The second time was when Carmella had tried to speak to another girl, a young, blond haired Westerner in a neighboring cell. Communication between prisoners was strictly forbidden. Fifteen strokes with a thin riding crop across her naked buttocks and thighs. Carmella thus knew that the five cracks she had just been given were only an appetizer compared to what the matron was capable of serving out. She obeyed fastidiously.

When she had removed all of her clothes, including the bra and panties that they had permitted her for her trial, she stood expectantly. She had not been permitted her Western clothes while awaiting trial and she knew not to expect them now. But something, a cheap cotton dress, a robe, something, these had always been supplied. But now, something else was happening. The matrons grabbed her arms and pulled them before her, clasping a pair of manacles around her wrists. A gag was forced into her mouth and tied tightly behind her head. Bending her over, they pushed her into a cage. As the door was shut, her hands were pulled through a small gap in the bars and fastened there with a leather strap. Carmella was thus forced to her knees in the tiny cage, kneeling on the wooden platform that served as its base. Her wrists were pinioned to the bars, leaving her hands dangling outside of the cage.

The matrons withdrew silently, extinguishing the light as they left. Carmella wailed bitterly, but silently, behind her gag. "Oh Jeb, where are you, what are you doing now? How could you have left me here?" she asked herself. How had her life come to this? What would happen to her now? She had been raped, humiliated, kept prisoner in a stark, silent prison, and now, sentenced. She shook her hands, which dangled just beyond the bars, pulling futilely at the cage door. Darkness had swallowed her. What would happen now?

It seemed an hour, maybe more before the door to the room opened again. The light at first blinded Carmella as she turned her head to see who had entered. Since she had been pinioned facing the far wall, she had to turn almost completely around to see. It was the matrons, this time hauling in a small blond girl; the same one Carmella had tried to talk to weeks earlier. She was sure it was the same girl. The girl was crying, but did not speak. Her long hair fell across her shoulders as she bent her head and sobbed silently. The guards quickly had her undress, as naked as Carmella. She was pale as the limestone walls of the prison cell, thin, but well endowed. She looked up briefly at Carmella, her eyes widening as she saw for the first time what was in store for her. Deftly the matrons gagged and bound the young blond girl and shoved her into the cell next to Carmella. As soon as she was bound to the cage door in the same manner as Carmella, the matrons left and the lights again went out.

In the darkness, Carmella could hear the muffled moaning of her companion. She wondered what crime the girl had committed. No doubt of the same degree and provenance as Carmella's 'crimes': being left vulnerable and defenseless in this medieval, cruel land.

Three more times the matrons came in, each time towing along one or more young girls, until the seven cages were full. Seven young females, bound and gagged, naked, helpless, were left to moan and cry in the darkness. Three of the condemned women were European, or at least Caucasian. The others were Asian, either Indian or Filipino, judging by their brown skin and black hair.

Carmella lost track of all time. Left there for several hours, she could no longer control her needs and had peed on the wooden floor of her cage. From the smells around her, so had several of her companions. The room began to stink of urine, sweat and fear. Her mouth was dry. Her stomach, empty since the meager breakfast, growled and pained her. Her knees ached from their contact with the floor, her back, strained at kneeling, was cramping, the pain stabbing through her. How long, how long? What was happening? How long could they keep her this way?

Suddenly the lights came on again. Three men entered the room. Many times during her imprisonment, Carmella had been forced to wait naked, or nearly so, while the matrons took their time in locking and unlocking the many doors between the cells and the various facilities, the toilets, the showers, the medical office. But there were no men in the women's jail. While it was apparently fair game to rape and torture defenseless women on the street and then arrest them for being victims of these same crimes, the jails themselves countenanced no sexual exploitation, by men at least. Carmella had wondered when several times women from neighboring cells had been summoned at strange hours, returning only hours later, red eyed and silent.

But here were men, Western dressed, uniformed, strolling into this women's detention area without hesitation or comment. Clearly the rules had changed. Again.

One of the men went to the wall and dragged out a hose. Turning it on, he washed down the women in the cages. The water was cold, but strangely refreshing. Each woman was doused for a full minute, the bottom of her cage rinsed. The second man followed the first toweling down the hands, which extended as if in prayer from each cell. He smiled and nodded to each woman, slowing to admire her breasts or flanks. The little ceremony appeared strange to Carmella until she saw what the third man had brought with him. Plugged into the wall opposite the cages, was a long, iron bar with a long cord that gave ample play for it to reach each cage. It was wrapped with some kind of heatproof cloth, the end beginning to glow red, red as the grill on a stove. This man too, smiled.

Carmella was first in line and first to feel the kiss of the branding iron. Placed on the flesh between her thumb and forefinger on her right hand, the rod burned deeply. Carmella screamed behind her gag. Her hand, held fast by the other two guards, burned as the fire was sunk into her. Carmella lost all control of herself screaming silently behind her gag and twisting and writhing within her tiny cage as the pain coursed through her. Her mind went blank but for the sheer pain of the biting iron. She hardly noticed as one of the men, after admiring his partner's handiwork smeared a green salve upon the fresh and angry wound. A small bandage was placed atop it. Although the pain made the moment of searing flesh seem eternal, it was actually done quite quickly. Ten minutes and the whole procedure was over for seven new convicts, marked for ownership by order of the State. Their business done, the three guards turned off the light, and left.

The marking of the hand was a quite efficient way to mark female prisoners in a country where most of the women covered their entire bodies whenever they emerged in public. A simple examination of the hand, "Madame would you please remove your glove?" would suffice to return the escaping convict to her chains. The brand was small, the coat of arms of the Emir, their formal owner as sentenced felons. His ownership entailed the right to use and dispose of his property as he wished. But all this was still in the future. For now, the women, recently sentenced, presently marked as chattel, knelt in their cages, their hands burning in pain, gagged and naked in the darkness, unaware of what their next encounter would bring.

It was with a different outlook that the women greeted the next opening of the door to the room untold hours later. The three men again. What would they do? What ordeal was next? Carmella's hands were loosened from the cage door and the door opened. She trembled with fear as she was pulled from the cage. She was allowed to straighten slowly, the men slapping her thighs and back to return the circulation of blood. She was led to the corner of the room where, squatting down over a small hole in the floor, she was permitted to pee and evacuate her bowels. She was then washed over by the hose again. This time she was rubbed with a soapy sponge. Her injured hand stung fiercely from the water, but the joy of standing upright and being free of the stink that had enveloped her in her cage made the pain bearable. The green salve was again applied to her tortured hand and another small bandage was placed over it. Carmella had no way of knowing, but the green salve served two purposes. It was, indeed, an antibiotic cream. But the green color was designed to seep into the burns of the hand. The symbol of the Emir, the wingspread falcon, would stand out, green hued. Hard to miss.

Carmella was then toweled down and led to the wall behind the cages, her wrists affixed to a ring on the wall slightly over her head. Her hair, which had also been washed, was brushed roughly, until the knots and tangles were worked out. Her gag was removed briefly and she was permitted to drink from a large brown bottle. The liquid was sweet and syrupy, but she was permitted her fill and, after several hours of thirst, it was refreshing. She was then regagged and left standing at the wall until each girl was serviced in turn.

The three men worked quickly and expertly. They smiled, prodded a breast here and there and even stroked one or two of the women between the legs. But otherwise, they completed their tasks in a most businesslike way.

It took less than an hour to cleanse the seven women. When they were all finished, they were released from the wall, one by one, their hands bracleted behind their backs. The liquid must have contained some form of soporific since Carmella felt her head begin to clog. She stumbled slightly as she was pulled towards the door of the room. Chains had been affixed to the bindings around her wrists and ran from there to the ankles of the woman behind her, and so on. A chain had been affixed between each woman's ankles, permitting only the tiniest of steps. The women limped forward slowly as they were led from the cell into the corridor. Down the corridor they went, shuffling like a perverse conga line, fear still in their eyes, cold, still aching from hours of confinement.

At the end of the corridor they were led into another room. This one was carpeted, actually plush. The lighting was dim compared to the stark corridor. Carmella struggled to make out the details of the room, her mind thick, her body trembling with cold and fear. She couldn't help remark to herself the irony of being chilled in the desert, the air conditioning blowing strongly from vents above. The women were led into to the middle of the room. There, seven chains fell from the ceiling, each about three feet apart, forming a small circle. Carmella was led to the farthest chain, the coffle of girls following behind her. She was freed from the coffle and her ankles unfettered. Her wrists were then affixed to the chain, which was pulled taut just enough to raise her arms behind her back, forcing her to bend her torso slightly forward. Her breasts swayed gently as her bent torso caused them to fall freely away from her chest. As each woman was similarly affixed, their ankles were freed only to be chained to the ankle of the woman on either side. Their legs were thus spread apart, straining their arm and shoulder muscles, as their wrists were pulled even further upwards behind them. The right ankle of the last woman, a tiny black haired girl, her eyes large, wide with fear, was anchored to Carmella's left.

Carmella's view was of a set of overstuffed chairs set against the wall opposite her. A small bar sat to the left, a door to the right. This was not the door they had used to enter the room and Carmella speculated that it led to the outside of the jail. As she wondered which door she would leave the room by, one of the guards appeared before her and from a small bundle under his left arm pulled forth a black hood. Carmella gasped, as well as she could with her mouth stuffed full of leather. The very idea of being hooded was abhorrent to her. She had been hooded before, while a prisoner of the men who had arrested her. The confinement, the powerlessness, the fear of suffocation pushed all of her reserve aside. She bobbed and weaved her head, moaning, calling out in her mind her entreaties, "Please don't do this, please don't, oh God, please!" Her motions set all the chained women in motion as Carmella pulled the girls to her left and right off balance.

Carmella's efforts were without avail as the guard pulled the hood over her head and yanked the drawstring tight around her neck. Carmella could hear him laugh and call out to the other guards his amusement. Carmella did all that she could to catch her breath. Breathing only through her nose, she steadied herself and pulled air as deeply as she could into her lungs. Don't panic, don't panic. They want you alive, you must stay alive, do anything, just live, she thought. Her mind raced as she felt the pull and tug of the other women as they too were hooded.

When the guards were done, they stepped back to admire their handiwork. A circle of flesh, all desirable, all available, their intimate parts displayed and presented. No time to dawdle though. Sooner or later these women, most, if not all, would be made available for their pleasure. Down the road, all of the slaves became available; time and abuse took their toll. Now these women were, for the most part, near the peak of their desirability. Training and some small adjustments to their appearances would bring them to their apogee. A tuck here, some weight loss there, maybe an implant, and soon these women would be servicing the rich and powerful of the kingdom. But then, later, well, there were the workingmen's brothels, and before that the minor officials', the strong-arms of the jails and police force, the enforcers of the might of the Emir, they would have their day. For now though, a caress, a grope was all that was permitted.

One of the men, the same who had passed out the hoods, stopped by Carmella as he readied himself to exit the room. He cupped her breasts in his hands, feeling their fullness and softness, the nipples hard and taut with fear. Carmella's chest rose and fell, giving her breasts life. He cooed to her softly, which, strangely enough, calmed her, her breathing easing, her trembling coming to a halt. She would live. She would, she thought. The warmth of the hands caressing her breasts told her that she was desired, valued. She would live.

Carmella heard the door to the room slam shut. Only the moaning and whimpering of her fellow captives disturbed the quiet of the room. She assumed they had been brought here to be displayed, abused, but she resisted in her mind the possible meanings of the peculiar arrangement in the room. Why would seven women be so brazenly displayed? Not to be sold, not that, that couldn't be it. Some bizarre ritual perhaps? Maybe the beginning of seventeen years of victimization within the prison system? Perhaps some form of initiation of the condemned? But sold, no, not that, not in this day and age. Slavery was abolished, wasn't it?

After a brief period, the door opposite Carmella opened. She could hear male voices, pleasant, amused, voices. A chair was moved, a cigar lit; she could smell it even through the hood. The sound of the stricken match was not unlike the rending of clothes. Ice in a glass. Her ears were alerted to every minute sound. More men came in. Was that French being spoken? She could feel a body approach hers. A finger grazed her breast, touched her nipple softly. She tried to straighten up, to pull away, but the motion strained her already aching arms and shoulders. Her bound legs gave her no leverage. A hand now cupped her left breast. She felt it raised slightly, warmth on the nipple, lips, a tongue. She could feel the pull in her womb as the mouth sucked on her breast gently. A voice spoke; her breast was released. More laughter. The sounds of men, powerful, self-confident men.

Carmella could sense the men as they stepped past her. She could hear the soft moan of a girl, apparently being caressed to arousal. Her own pussy was warm and moist. Her body was anticipating a sensual experience. Were these men going to fuck them? For now, anyway, they were clearly inspecting the lot of goods before them. Suddenly the meeting was apparently called to order since there was the banging of a hammer on wood, perhaps a gavel, and then silence. Carmella felt herself being shifted to her right. She then realized that the chains were on some kind of wheel, allowing the women to be displayed one at a time to the men standing before them. Carmella could hear a voice murmuring, the shuffle of chains, a woman's gasp, some chatter, a decision? Something had been decided, the chain moved on. Carmella shuffled her feet to her right once more, then four more times as each girl was inspected in turn. Once, a girl began to plead, beg, apparently her gag having been removed. A slap, two, then only whimpering, soon muffled again. Silence was required of prisoners.

And then it was her turn. Carmella felt her breasts being measured, weighed, by several sets of hands. Her legs, already parted, were invaded, her vagina stroked and, penetrated. Even her rear was fondled, probed, the tightness of her thigh muscles tested, the flab, small as it was, grabbed on her hips. And then her hood was removed. Three men stood before her, one behind them. One of the men was holding a file, apparently a dossier of some sort. There was her picture on top, her mug shot, a narrative of some kind. A picture fell from the file to the floor at her feet. A woman was on her knees; a cock was in her mouth, a blindfold over her eyes. She knelt on a bed her hands fastened to her waist. The man lay beneath her, his legs spread, the picture ending at his middle. Carmella felt nauseous. It was her, in the hotel. She remembered now vaguely, someone had been taking pictures. Oh, God, how many pictures? Who had them? Her eyes were diverted from this tableau as a hand encircled her face, grabbing her cheeks, forcing her head up. He made some comment to the others, more laughter. Her gag was undone, removed, her mouth opened, probed by fingers. The men conversed, the gag and the hood returned, the decision made.

A good half hour passed without much further action. The ache in Carmella's arms had turned into a dull, throbbing pain. The gags and hoods stifled the women's soft moans and cries of pains, emitting occasionally only the most desperate cry, and that only as a muffled whimper. She could hear the rustle of the chains as the captives swayed back and forth or side-to-side to ease their discomfort. The balls of Carmella's feet were on fire as she leaned forwards onto her toes, trying to mitigate the pressure on her arms from the chain that pulled them up behind her.

She could hear the faint sound of paperwork being shuffled, the sound of drinks being poured and downed, funny stories being finished. Men at play and work. Men who loved their work, worked at their play. Men who used women, owned them, enslaved them. Here they were deciding the fate of the latest batch. “Oh please, if you like her you must have her.” “Oh, no, you are too kind, I know you appreciate her, I'll take the brunette with the small breasts. I like long legs.” “The pale one for me, the blond, I can use her I'm sure.” “Well then it’s settled, have another drink and tell me about your golf trip to Scotland.” And on and on. Men who dealt with each other all the time. “Today I give you the pick of the litter, next time it's mine.” Somewhere, in the days to come, money would be transferred from account to account, anonymous, nameless accounts, their owners names reduced to codes and numbers, as the women here today were reduced, their names and their personalities to be submerged into their new roles as property.

CHAPTER SIX

After about an hour, the sounds of the men subsided. Carmella heard the opening and shutting of doors, the shuffling of chairs. Thereafter, a brief pause, and the still hooded women were released from the chains and formed up in a line. As each was released, a small band was fastened around her neck. The band held a small disk that contained their assigned number and their destination. Carmella, still hooded, felt herself pulled forward, her feet shuffling, limited by the chains which linked her ankles and joined her to the women to her front and rear.

A short walk through the door from whence they had come and down the hall and the women were led into yet another room. Here they were made to stand as each in her turn was released from her ankle fetters, placed in a chair and one of her legs raised in a stirrup. The right ankle was affixed by means of a leather strap, as was the thigh. Each female squirmed and moaned as her new number was tattooed onto her foot, on the side, just above the arch. The pinpricks were painful, burning, but tolerable. The man was skilled and finished quickly. Carmella cried bitterly to herself as the needles were jammed home. Confined and hooded as she was, it would be some time before she would know what had been done to her foot. For now she imagined it to be simply another torture inflicted on her at the whims of her new masters. But, rather, this was the way that her physical person would be tracked within the system, her number to match her document, the Certificate of Enslavement, which had been signed earlier that day. As she passed henceforth from user to user, as she served her sentence and worked off her debt to the State, this number would connect her to the system, confirm her status, locate her presence in the gulag to which she had been condemned.

Some of the women would be marked more specifically once they had reached their training houses. One house had its seal burned into the flesh between the cheeks of the slave's posterior. Another tattooed the skin surrounding the areola of the breasts with a red dye as well as the lips of the vagina, which were then left shaved. Most common was the addition of a brand to the left hand, marking the name of the house on the slave. The houses were proud of their work, and wanted their skills well advertised. Likewise, some of the houses specialized their training so that one house produced slaves whose rear openings were as dexterous and agile as lips, another taught exquisite oral skills, another bred pairs who would delight the viewer with their displays of Sapphic lust.

There were 10 main houses for the training, abuse and use of slaves in the country and fifteen or so minor ones. They obtained their raw material not only through the courts of the Emirate, as in the case of Carmella, but also through the various channels of illegitimate commerce that circled the globe. Thus a shop girl in Brussels, a model in Milan, a peasant girl from Asia, Africa or South America, any young woman who happened to fall astray of the thousands of gangsters, hoodlums or men of power who were plugged into this underworld Internet, could find herself "stung on the hand" as the slavers jokingly put it. Transported by plane and ship, overnight or over the course of days or even weeks, the girls would find themselves on their knees, the arms pinned behind them, nude, awaiting the pleasure of a master.

Hundreds of women every year were processed through these training centers. For while they served as training houses for the newly enslaved, the houses also served as markets for the old, the used, retrained and refitted for a new master. In the meantime, and as they awaited disposition, the girls served the visitors of the houses as would any whore. But these whores were owned. You could rent them for an hour, an evening or for a month. In fact, the ownership of the slaves never really passed from the state. They were leased by the houses and, in turn, rented out to those who desired them. A month, a year, a week, all these were possible. And if you could not take them out of the country, or even out of the special zone in the interior where these activities were confined, this served the Emirate well since the wealthiest of the world's thieves, murderers, scoundrels, and yes, merely powerful, sought fit to live or vacation there, feeding a stream of revenue to the Crown through their vices.

Carmella's fate was to be contracted to one of the smaller houses. Its renown was not through specialization of its training, but in its thoroughness. Only the most desirable women were selected, and then, only ones of intelligence and refinement, ones who would better understand the subtleties and ironies of their training.

These women knew what it was to be an object of desire, but yet remote, unattainable to most. They remained desirable, even more so, since now they were clearly attainable only to someone with either the cash or the juice to be admitted to the house's salons and boudoirs, or to be 'leased', essentially owned, subject to the slightest caprice or whim of their masters.

But this elegance, this refinement in both carriage and technique, sexual technique that is, was obtained at a dear price, a price paid wholly by the slave. While other houses sought compliance, obedience, acquiescence, the House of Adeem sought more. Total, absolute acceptance of their status as slaves was demanded and, usually, achieved. This entailed the total submersion of personality, total commitment to the pleasure of others and a total immersion in sensuality, both pain and pleasure. These women were not so much trained as reshaped, remolded. The prices they commanded were the highest, but deservedly so. All this was achieved through the absolute destruction of the personality of the subject and their total recreation as a creature of pleasure. If the raw material was there, the end result was almost perfection. If not, well, there was ample room in the dungeons of the Emir for disposal of the broken, the maimed and the useless. In fact, the occasional torture to the death of a subject provided great motivation to those still in training and was insurance against backsliders.

Carmella had little inkling of this future as she was trundled down the corridor after her marking and placed back in the cage she had left a short while before. An hour, maybe two, passed, and the cages were cleared as the new masters of these women's flesh claimed their goods. Voices, men's of course, the slamming of cell doors, the tinkling of chains, all assaulted Carmella's ears as she knelt, naked and hooded, trembling, awaiting her fate. Suddenly it was her turn. Her cage door opened, and she was lifted out. Her hands were chained together and locked behind her back. Still hooded and gagged, she was pulled by a chain hooked to a steel collar that had been snapped around her neck, and shuffled off to her future.

Carmella was not alone on her chain. She could feel a tug on a chain on the back of her collar as she was hustled along the corridor. She had little time or energy to speculate which one of the women was coffled with her. Her ankles were still hobbled by a short chain and she had to shuffle her legs quickly to avoid falling. Suddenly, she stopped, an elevator, down, and then walking again, then some stairs, a platform. The texture of the floor had changed from the cool smoothness of the tiled floors to a rough concrete finish. Her feet were scuffed as she stumbled to keep up with the pull of the chain beneath her chin. She could hear the sounds of cars, vans, whatever, their engines idling. After a moment's hesitation, a van door slid open. Hands released the chains that bound her to her companion. Still with her hands joined behind her back, Carmella was pulled inside the van and pushed down to the floor. Her breasts were crushed against the coarse carpet. Carmella felt her companion forced down beside her. Her ankles were drawn together, the chain between them shortened and then connected to her wrists. The van door closed, the front door opened and shut, the engine revved, and it sped away.

The full terror of her situation now struck Carmella. She was naked, bound and gagged, being carted away to God knew where. Although in jail up to now, she had at least been in contact with the world outside. She had received a heavily censored letter from Jeb, a visit from the Embassy, another letter from her mother and father. They knew where she was. And although she didn't know exactly where the jail stood in the city, she knew it was within a short drive from her hotel, the airport. Now, she was riding a bullet to obscurity. How would anyone find her to help her? How would she contact the world? What was really happening here? Was it really what it seemed? Was there another end to this story than the one she now believed and feared?

The brand on her hand still stung, as did the tattoo on her foot. Her mouth and throat were dry. Again she had to pee and the muscles in her arms and legs ached from their confinement. The van jolted back and forth along the roads as the driver sped along at a typical third world reckless pace. Carmella could hear the city beyond the confines of the van, the beeping of horns, the screeching of brakes. At one point she actually heard voices as the van apparently stopped at a traffic light. English speaking voices, a man's and a woman's. The woman was laughing. Carmella could not make out enough words to make sense of the conversation as it quickly faded away. But the meaning of what she heard was clear. There was still a world out there where a woman could laugh, speak freely, walk in the sun.

Carmella felt a wave of self pity and sorrow spread over her. She could hear her own muffled sobs as her chest heaved and her body shivered. Her hood was loose enough so that she could feel the tears fall down her cheeks. But yet, after a few moments, she rallied herself. Survive, she thought, survive. That was all that mattered. She would do what she was told, obey, do anything, so that someday she could again laugh, feel the free breeze on her face, determine her own fate. She must survive.

The two women spent about five hours traveling in the van. The driver stopped twice to permit the women to attend nature's needs. This was done at the side of the road, the women squatting in the dust, the driver, heedless of the occasional passing car or truck. What a vision for the casual passer by, two women, naked, hooded, their arms bound, squatting like dogs on a leash. Would anyone in this hard, hard land care?

A squirt on the ground, a gulp of water, then back in the van, regagged, hooded and off to their unknown destination. Carmella let the rhythm of the road lull her. They were out of the city now, smooth macadam beneath their wheels. She could hear the hum of the tires and the drone of the engine. The driver had some Arabic station on, the music shrill and tinny, like some warped incarnation of rock and roll. Finally, Carmella felt the van reduce speed. A short stop, voices, then the van started again, slowly, like entering some kind of a gaited enclave. Carmella's hunch was right and the van pulled off of the desert road and coasted slowly over a gravel path. She heard the sound of a gate or large door opening, the van pulled forward again slowly and then halted once more.

Unknown hands lifted her and pulled her from the van. Her ankle bonds were loosened and she was allowed to test her legs for a moment, waking them from their slumber. Then, a chain was affixed to her neck and she was bound again to her unknown companion and pulled forward. The gravel pricked the soles of her feet as she walked. Twenty, maybe twenty five steps, still gagged and hooded, she was pulled forward, and then down a short flight of stairs. Night or day, she wasn't sure. The stones were hot, but her skin seemed cool, like the coolness of the desert at night. A door opened and shut and she was pulled further along a corridor, down some more stairs and then through another series of doors.

Throughout this short trip she was not permitted to rise to her full height. Rather, the chain to her collar was grabbed close to her neck and pulled down to the waist of her escort. When she finally was permitted to halt, she could feel her collar being affixed to some kind of post or bar. She had been released from the other unfortunate woman somewhere along the way. Her legs were spread apart and her ankles chained to the floor. Some kind of stanchion or stool was placed at her waist. Thus, she was bent over, her sex and rear exposed, unable to kneel or rest on the floor. For a short while there was silence and then, a whistling sound.

Carmella was immediately able to identify the sound since it culminated in a searing pain to the back of her legs. She was whipped repeatedly up and down the length of her legs and buttocks. She screamed sharply behind her gag and tried to twist and turn to avoid the blows. But the man at the other end of the whip knew his business and each stroke was delivered on target. It was a thin leather covered reed, not unlike a riding crop, and it left thin, bright red welts everywhere it touched.

Carmella was too deeply engaged in screaming and the experience of the pain of the blows to notice at first that the blows had stopped. Neither did she hear the door open and close again. But when she did come to her senses, she realized that she was alone. And she stayed alone. Two, three, maybe four hours, she could not tell. Her legs and rear burned from the whipping. Her legs and back ached from the cruel position she had been left in. Her mouth and lips were raw from the gag, her throat constricted and dry. Her arms, strained by the clasps that held her wrists bound behind her, ached. Her feet had been rubbed raw by the concrete floor in her effort to dodge the blows of the whip. Carmella could tell nothing about the room in which she was confined and could hear little of what was going on beyond the large door that she had heard clang shut when she had been first brought in. A door slamming, a man's laugh, a woman's desperate pleas and subsequent screams, was all she heard faintly through the door.

Hours later, Carmella was finally freed, a man's hands lifting her off of the stanchion on which he torso had rested. She was allowed to stand for a moment and then was dragged over to the corner of the room. Pushed down into a squat, she understood she was to pee and did so gratefully. Her hood was lifted and her gag removed long enough to permit her to drink from a flask pushed between her lips. She drank desperately, her throat screaming with joy.

She was not permitted a view of the room as the hood was pulled up only just enough to expose her mouth. Suddenly, the gag and hood were replaced. She tried to beg, "No, no, I'll do what ever you want, please," but her voice was muffled as the leather plug was sent home. She was pushed to her knees, her hands freed from behind her only to be affixed before her and then to a chain, pulling her backwards over some kind of stool or ottoman. Her ankles were again affixed to the floor and a strap was pulled around her waist and, fastened to the object below her, her body now almost bowed. A pause, and again the whistling sound and the crack of a whip's contact with flesh echoed through the room. Her breasts and belly were now subjected to the punishing blows she had first felt on her rear and the backs of her legs.

For two days the rain of blows continued intermittently. Never was a word spoken to her and neither was she permitted to speak. Every part of her body was in turn repeatedly subjected to its quota. Her breasts and belly, the insides of her thighs as she lay with her legs spread akimbo, the front of her thighs as she was stood on her toes her hands high above her, her back, her arms, her feet, her backside and then, around the horn again. Even her outstretched palms were tortured, the pain shooting up her arms. The beatings came in no particular order and at varying intervals. An hour, three, five. Fifteen minutes more than once. A rain of blows designed to maximize the terror of her confinement. The instruments of her debasement varied as well, a riding crop, a many tailed whip, an actual lash, all these and more raised welts and bruises on her otherwise pastel flesh. Each time she was left in the position in which she had been beaten, a reminder that more was to come.

More than once Carmella gave up hope of life as the whips stung her again and again. "They are killing me bit by bit," she thought frantically. "I'm lost. Dead." She mixed prayers with her silent pleas for mercy.

This intense initiation to pain and the mercilessness of her captors was designed to drive all hope of rescue or respite from the new slave. Deprived of any sense of time, driven to levels of pain previously not even dreamed of, all rationality was lost. Only a quivering, helpless mass remained. Carmella had no inkling when her initiative punishment was finally ended. She had been left kneeling on the hard stone, bent over backwards over an ottoman, her sex and thighs having been given a dozen hearty strokes a few hours before. When the door opened, Carmella's heart began to pound. Her body convulsed with fear. Her throat was thick. Just the desired effect of her treatment. Desperate to avoid the unavoidable, she tried mentally to hide her body within itself, to shrink beyond detection, to vanish, to disappear.

Carmella felt her hands and ankles freed from the rings on the floor, her body pulled up off of the ottoman. She expected the worse and had already started to whine and cringe. Suddenly, unexpectedly, her hood was lifted. The dim light of the room was blinding to her at first, her hair matted against her head. The gag was likewise removed. Carmella was standing, sagging really, her hands reaffixed behind her back, leaning against the bulky male who had freed her. Could it be that the whippings were done? Was her ordeal over? Had she survived? She looked at the man's face. Not necessarily cruel, but solid, forceful, demanding. She tried to speak, but her lips trembled uncontrollably, her voice refusing to come. "Thank you," she wanted to say. "Thank you for this moment's respite, this moment's peace." A bottle was forced to her lips; she drank. Her head began to swim. She passed out.

When she awoke, many hours later, Carmella found herself locked in a small cage located in the corner of the room which had been her prison for the last several days. She could see the room clearly now. It was about 400' square, bare concrete walls and floor. The instruments of her torture were strewn around the room, the stanchion, the ottoman, the rings in the floor, a set of stocks that had held her confined in various positions for many hours. At the far end, near the thick wooden door, were several large pillows, suitable for reclining. Along the wall was mounted a series of whips, ropes, cuffs and other forms of confinement or debasement. A shower and toilet sat in the corner opposite the cage, unadorned, unshielded from view.

Carmella took in her surroundings as she took stock of herself, slowly coming out of her coma-like sleep. She realized that she had probably been drugged. Her arms were no longer pinioned behind her. Her whole body ached and she tried to stretch out to the limits of her cage. As she did so, she discovered that her wrists were bound to her sides by thick leather bracelets clipped to a wide leather belt around her waist. Cramped by the tiny cage, she could not stretch out to her full length. As she struggled to a sitting position she noticed for the first time that her pubis had been shaved. Viewing her lower lips so prominently displayed startled her, but not as much as her next discovery. As she shook her head to stretch her neck and relieve the cramps in her jaw something was missing. She shook her head again. Her hair! On her head! It was gone! Her beautiful, long brown hair! Jeb used to love to run his fingers through it. She had treasured her twice-daily ritual of brushing it, a hundred strokes, morning and night. During her pretrial imprisonment she had been calmed and comforted by this routine connecting her to her life outside. Now even this was to be denied to her.

The purpose of the acts of cruelty against her, the beatings and confinement were now clear to her. She was an object, an owned thing, an animal. She was being broken to her new life, being deprived of her own will. All that was formerly hers, every aspect of herself, now belonged to some faceless other or others. A terrible thought now crept into her mind. What if they did not want to possess her, to use her at all? What if this was what they wanted, to torment her, to inflict cruelty after cruelty upon her until she could physically withstand no more and died? She wanted to live. She wanted to survive. But how could she if the pleasures that her body offered were of no value, if she had no ability to barter with her new masters, their pleasure for her life?

All of this uncertainty and torment was exactly the point of the initiation Carmella had received. She was to be totally and absolutely mastered, with nothing left for her but the need to avoid pain. The idea that she would be able to barter any part of herself for a benefit from her new masters was to be driven from her mind. She was to be totally committed to obedience, to opening herself, serving the wants of her masters, without reservation, without hope of reward. Her only motivation would be to avoid a return to this dungeon in which she now was now entombed. She would divest herself of all that she had been, or she would die.

Carmella cried out, a long, wailing loud groan, wracked by sobs which shook her whole body. "No, no, no!" she cried. "What's to become of me? What have I done? Oh, please, please, don't do this to me, please!" Her voice echoed off of the walls of her prison cell. She did not know who she was calling to. Only the stone walls could hear her. She had no reason to believe that anyone, even if they could hear her plaintive wails, would help her. It was the need inside her for pity, for an end to her torment, that cried out. She began to weep silently.

Carmella had no idea how long she had been in the cell, how long she had been in the cage or how long she had been awake. After her outburst, she seemed to drift in and out of slumber, waking with a start occasionally as the faint sounds from beyond her door reached her. The light, though dim, left the room bright enough so that any distinction between night and day was impossible. She still hadn't eaten since breakfast the day of court, however long ago that was. Her whole body was raw from punishment. She could see the stripes left behind by the whips, the black and blue from the heavier canes that had been used. When she finally heard the door being unlocked and opened, her heart jumped into her throat. What would it be this time? Was her respite from beatings over? What new torture would she face?

The man who entered was the man she had seen when her hood and gag had been removed. He was heavy set, tall, brawny. His features were hard, his eyes steely gray. He was wearing a pair of grey gym shorts, sandals and nothing else. He was young, in his twenties, not much over twenty-five. He looked hard.

The man said nothing to Carmella as he entered the room. He slammed the door shut and hung the keys on a nail by the door. He looked at Carmella briefly and then walked over to the toilet. He pulled his cock out of the shorts and pissed into the bowl, closing his eyes as he emptied himself. Carmella stared at his organ; wide and long, it filled the man's hand. She sensed that she would soon be better acquainted with it herself.

The man shook his cock, shedding the last few drops of water into the toilet, pushed a button that flushed it and turned to the cage holding Carmella. Slowly he ranged his eyes over her flesh, from her face to her breasts, to her naked sex below. Carmella trembled as she felt the power and ruthlessness of his gaze. She knew that this man had been certainly responsible for much, if not all, of her torment of the past few days. She had never felt so helpless in her life. Her breathing became short and labored as she held back her panic. He had done no more than stare at her and already her flesh was tight with fear, her mouth dry, her hands and armpits wet with perspiration. The man seemed to come to some decision. He reached up to a hook on the wall and pulled down a key which he used to unlock the door to the cage. Carmella cringed away from the door. She knew that only pain could await her outside of her cage and she had no desire to facilitate it. That was until the man said one word, "Out!" His voice was the voice of command.

Carmella quickly crawled out of the cage, slithered, actually, since with her wrists pinioned to her hips, they could not support her. The man held a small quirt in his hand and tapped her with it on her back and rear until she was centered in the room. He pulled her to her knees, and, again with the quirt, lifted her chin until she was raised to her maximum height. He then slapped at her thighs until her legs were spread wide, and then pushed her backwards until she was resting on her heels.

Tears were streaming down Carmella's face. All of her wanted to cry out to beg for mercy, to stay the blows, the torment she knew was coming. But she had not been given permission to speak and somehow she knew that speaking without permission from this lurking, hulk of a man would initiate her pain. By sheer act of will, she held herself in, her body trembling, her eyes glued to the monster who held her in his thrall.

The man sat cross-legged before her, the whip held across his lap, staring into her eyes. Finally, after many minutes, he spoke. Carmella jumped at the sound of his voice.

"Today is the first day of your training as a body slave. My name is Aboud. Your name is Slave. Before I inflict today's discipline I will explain to you the rules of your training. You shall, first of all, obey all commands quickly, without reservation and completely. This will not free you from the infliction of bodily pain, which is an important part of your training, but failure in this regard will surely prolong it, intensify it and increase its frequency. Continued failure to obey satisfactorily will mean termination of your training and your execution. By a very painful process, I might add. Do you understand so far?"

Carmella's face was contorted in a paroxysm of grief and terror. She nodded hurriedly.

"The second rule is that you must remain silent at all times. Cries and screams do not count. Besides, during punishments you will usually be gagged. But pleas for mercy, begging for release, the cessation of the punishment, anything of a similar manner will not be tolerated. Do you understand?"

She understood the words. But she felt difficulty in comprehending what was being said. Training? For what? Was she condemned to being a beaten, tortured chattel, or was there more? What chances would she have to emerge from her chamber of horrors?

Aboud seemed to read her mind. "It is not for you to try to guess how to act or to try to impress me or one of the other trainers. It is your very will which is to be broken.

You will be taught to serve and obey your masters. As we find it pleasing to use your body, we shall do so. You will give yourself to this, your only real duty. When you have been sufficiently trained you will be permitted to serve those whom we will permit access to you. Your only role in life is to obey. You are now a slave, owned by the Emir, and will be taught to obey without question, without reservation."

Aboud's eyes pierced Carmella's. Her breathing was heavy, labored, evidence of the panic which lay just beneath the surface. Desperately she fought off the urge to throw herself at this man's feet, to beg for mercy, to be freed, to end this nightmare. But she believed him when he told her that painful punishments awaited her. She could sense that this man was as hard and as cruel as the walls themselves, even worse, since the walls merely caused her pain, they did not lust for it. The walls and chains had no drive to dominate and crush her; they were just there, passive instruments of the will of others. This man who sat before her, his voice calm, his demeanor peaceful, his eyes like hot irons through her heart, he was the true threat, the true enemy. Her master.

Aboud was tapping the whip absentmindedly in his palm, his eyes piercing Carmella. Carmella knew that whip and would shortly know it again, this she was sure of. But it could be worse, so much worse. She struggled for composure. She could stop her voice, but not her tears. She expected no sympathy from the hulk before her, and knew that the chances were that her display of fear and sorrow would further entice this man, her trainer, as he called himself, to heights of cruelty. But something had broken inside her as she had heard the man's words, making explicit for the first time, her fate.

"You will now stand." The voice was soft and yet hard. A command. Carmella struggled to rise, her hands bound at her waist. She was forced to push up from the floor using only her legs. She stumbled as she gained her feet. The man released her hands from the belt around her waist and removed it. He attached Carmella's bracelets to a chain that hung from the ceiling. Carmella was certain she had been affixed to this chain before, looped through an iron ring in the stone above, but before she had been hooded, gagged. Now she would see the blows, the face of her tormentor. She shuddered and a small pitiful whine escaped her lips. She dared not speak, dared not beg for mercy. Nothing short of a miracle could prevent what was certainly about to occur. And miracles were outlawed by the Emir.

Aboud finished securing her wrist cuffs to the chain and proceeded to pull it taut. Carmella's arms were lifted above her head until the muscles were stretched taut, her heels lifted several inches off of the ground. Aboud tied off the chain on a hook on the wall and stepped over to his prisoner. He appraised her, her breasts, her thighs, good muscle tone there. Carmella's features were comely, even in her distress, and the man admired her smooth face, the elegance of her mouth and eyes. A very special catch, he thought. He stepped closer to the girl. He could see her trembling, lines of sweat forming in her armpits and slowly gliding down her sides to her hips and below. Facing Carmella, he lifted her left breast in his right hand, weighing it, caressing it softly. He ran his thumb over the nipple as he watched the reaction in the girl's face. She started slightly, betraying herself. Fear was exciting, even to the victim. Aboud bent over and took the nipple in his mouth. He sucked at it slowly, running his tongue over the nipple. He had wrapped his arm around the girl's waist and drawn her against his body. First one nipple, then the other, made tight and hard by the girl's involuntary responses.

Carmella felt her womb tighten at the ministrations to her breasts. A slow warmth built inside, gradually overcoming her fear. She felt herself sliding into a consciousness of pleasure and its possibilities that she had thought left behind. But this lapse was momentary as her hands writhed against the chains that held them aloft, as she strained to keep her balance on her toes. She could not forget where she was, what was about to happen. The sensations confused her though, frightened her, shamed her. She could not, must not, find pleasure amidst her torment. She must fight, she must survive.

The man raised his lips from the young woman's breast and looked into her face. He had felt her body soften and respond to his oral caress. "Oh, yes, this one is special," he thought. "A gift."

He slowly slid his hands down the girl's sides, feeling the concaveness of her waist, the pleasant outcrop of her hips. Her skin was almost white from the weeks of confinement, her tan faded. "Good," he told himself, "she will be soon be as white as alabaster." The welts and bruises, which already adorned her body, from knees to breasts, front and back, would stand out nicely. She would become a favorite, but he must deal with her correctly. Her training was everything.

Stepping back he saw the fear jump back into the girl's eyes. She was silent as she had been commanded, the strain of her obedience crisscrossing her face. Her baldness and the hairlessness of her body diminished Carmella beyond the not insignificant difference in her height from Aboud. Tears were streaming down her face. As Aboud reached for a long, narrow crop from the wall, Carmella suddenly lost all ability to control herself. Blubbering and crying, she begged for release, for mercy. Aboud frowned, disappointed. She will learn. From a rack on the wall he took a small rubber ball and a roll of tape. He stepped forward and slapped Carmella full cross the face, staggering her. She screeched loudly in pain as she swung wildly on her chain, hiding her face between her arms to avoid the next blow. But it did not come, Aboud merely placed his heavy, vice-like hand on her throat and squeezed.

Carmella gasped for breath, her eyes bugging out, her screams reduced to a gurgle as she was throttled. As she opened her mouth to gasp for air, Aboud dropped in the rubber ball. It was taped in place before Carmella knew what was happening. Although small in Aboud's hand, it filled her mouth, cutting off all air from that source, spreading her lips apart in a wide grimace. The tape held it firmly in place, wide enough to cover both her lips and down to her chin. Carmella strained to breathe through her nose, Aboud having released his grasp from her throat to apply the gag.

Without waiting for the girl to regain her composure, he took the crop from the floor where he had dropped it and let it whistle through the air. The first blow struck Carmella across her breasts. Her reaction was immediate as she moaned violently behind her gag. Another blow struck across her belly and another across the front of her thighs; seven blows in quick succession seared into her skin.

Aboud stepped back from his work, watching the girl

moan as she swung back and forth, hanging limp in her chains. He waited a few moments for the girl to catch her breath and he began again. Seven strokes, this time starting low on her legs, ascending to her thighs and her buttocks, each one leaving a strip of fire, a line of red. Five times altogether Aboud started and stopped the girl's torment. Each time there were seven blows struck. Each time he waited for the girl to cease dancing and writhing from the impact of the blows, to achieve respite. Thirty five times the crop whistled through the air, tearing at Carmella's skin. Thirty five times Carmella screamed out in pain, screams, however, that died in her throat.

Finally, he released Carmella's bonds and let her slump to the floor. As she lay weeping silently behind her gag, he paused to strip off his shorts. The workout had brought a fine sheen of sweat to his body. His cock was rampant, standing warlike at attention. Carmella looked up at her tormentor. No doubt what was coming next. The man motioned for her to rise, tapping the crop in his hand. Carmella rose slowly, first to her knees, and then nervously to her feet. Her breath was labored beneath the gag. Her face, streaked with tears, wincing and trembling as she steadied herself, able to look only at the floor below, awaiting a command.

Aboud took in the sight of the naked, terrified female before him. Despite the bruises and the lacerations, despite the shaved skull, the puffy eyes and cheeks, he could appreciate that Carmella was a morsel worth savoring. He walked around her, contemplating how best to use her. He stopped when behind her and stepped up to her so that his chest was pressed against her back. His arms circled her, replacing the leather belt that had previously been affixed there, reattaching her wrists to her waist.

Carmella first felt panic when Aboud stepped behind her and then relief from the pressure of his body against hers. She knew that no blow was imminent. His arms swallowed her as his right hand extended across her front to seize her left breast. The man's grasp was firm, without tenderness, and yet somehow soothing. She felt her nipple harden as he pressed its tip between his fingers. The other hand passed over her hip and pushed apart her thighs. There was no question what the man's goal was, but, rather than offending and tormenting her, the idea that the use of her body could distract him from his torment of her was, in an odd way, comforting. As he pressed his fingers at the gate of her sex, she widened her thighs, pressing herself into his hand, willing herself to please him, to help him find his delight.

The woman's cooperation in her ravishment did not go unnoticed by Aboud. This instinct for preservation was what was sought for in her training. She must be driven beyond the thought of bartering her charms for relief from ill treatment. No, this is what they wanted from her, a surrender of her will, an anticipation of her masters' desires. That alone would ameliorate her suffering. But not eliminate it, for who could forgo the pleasure of watching this beauteous creature dance to the whip.

Quickly, Aboud's fingers penetrated the outer lips of Carmella's sex. Deftly, he had fingered her cleft until the lubrication had started. He penetrated her to the full length of his fingers. With his other hand he caressed Carmella's breast, softly kneading her flesh, rolling her nipple between his fingers. For Carmella's part, this careful, almost tender manipulation was a sudden shock. She was smart enough to realize the lesson being taught. She knew that this hulk of a man was demonstrating his mastery of her. And she accepted it. Her lessons had been well taught. This moment called for pleasure, the next ...well she would think about that later.

Aboud's ministrations were having their effect on Carmella. She could feel the heat building up in her sex, her need for release surging, her breath shortening as she gave in to the flow of Aboud's caresses. With a swift and graceful sweep of his arms, Aboud suddenly lifted Carmella from her feet and carried her over to the small pallet that lay on the floor across from her cage. Aboud placed her down and lay atop her, pushing her legs apart with his knees. Carmella's hands strained at the belt around her waist. If her hands were free, would she have tried to push this devil away, or pulled him down onto her breasts? She didn't know. But she did know that whatever happened now, it was his choice, his will which controlled, his pleasure which was to be served.

Slowly, Aboud drew his cock to Carmella's sex, teasing the entrance, rubbing himself along the edges of the lips which he had parted just moments before. Carmella felt herself spinning wildly into heat, losing any thought of resistance, wanting only for this man to enter her to fill her, to push her to release. Aboud pushed slowly inside the panting woman, her breath hampered by her gag, causing her to draw air through her nose, snorting and wheezing with need. Her crevasse was hot and tight as Aboud drove his cock slowly home.

He had grabbed Carmella's face with his hands and held it close to his, his eyes boring into hers. Wide eyed, Carmella stared back into the cold, grey eyes of her lover, seeing deep within, her doom, her fate. She was lost now. She would do all she was asked, obey without question, endure all imposed. She begged, in her mind, for release. "Please, please take me there. Take me to that place where all else but the waves of pleasure will be gone."

Aboud, having mastered dozens of slaves before this one, having been taught his craft at the side of true masters, could read this woman's need. He could feel her rising to meet his thrusts. Slowly, surely, he built her passions beneath him. Pausing, starting again, thrusting deeply, then shallow, grinding his hips into hers, he played to her passion, letting his own need climb inexorably to its finish. Suddenly, knowing it was time, knowing that only this last thing was needed to seal this slave's fate, he let go, his cock throbbing, spurting, pumping his hot seed deep into her belly. Carmella felt his release, her own passion exploding as his hot fluids sank into her womb, his cock pulsing, whipping her into a furious arc of intensity.

For a few moments she lay beneath this giant, panting, recovering from this torrid flow of passion. Aboud, still hard, gently stroked his cock back and forth in the now fully bloomed sex beneath him. He could smell her secretions, the proof of her excitement. He knew he could easily force this now broken woman to another pitch of excitement, as he could feel her move her hips gently to the slow strokes of his cock. But not this time. For now, this slave would need some reinforcement of her abjectivity.

Carmella's eyes, squeezed shut during her moments of passion, remained shut as she felt the instrument of her pleasure sliding gently back and forth in her canal. Her body shuddered slightly as it recalled the throbs of pleasure that had overwhelmed it shortly before. Almost involuntarily, Carmella began to meet the rhythmic thrusts of her tormentor. Then suddenly, the gentle strokes to her pussy stopped. Suddenly, Carmella was recalled to where she was, what had been happening to her. Her eyes opened like a flash, only to find the black pupils of her master penetrating them.

Aboud slipped his cock from the prostrate woman and stood. As he did, he grabbed the still confined arms of his victim and lifted her to her feet. Her eyes widened as she anticipated her next round of torture. Her body was sweaty, her breath heavy. Drops of sweat rolled from her naked scalp down her forehead and into her eyes. She quaked with fear.

But further torment would be postponed, for now. Aboud had other plans. Carmella must be taught her vulnerability in more subtle fashions as well as the more emphatic. The ball gag was removed. Aboud gave Carmella a drink from a flask, water this time, no drugs. She was grateful for the relief it gave her. She stood silent and motionless as Aboud brought to the center of the room a small padded stool. Placing it on the floor before her, he motioned for Carmella to lower herself to her knees and to drape herself across it. Carmella did so, trembling in her recollection of the many beatings she had already received, undoubtedly some of it while extended across this very stool.

Her face was pointed away from the cell door and she could see her little cage before her. She yearned for its protection. She then felt her legs being drawn wide apart and her ankles fastened to rings in the floor. Since the stool was lower than her hips, her back arched invitingly, displaying her twin nether orifices nicely. Via a small chain,

Aboud fastened the collar around the woman's neck to a ring in the floor in front of the stool. The collar pulled Carmella's head downwards, so that her eyes could focus only on the floor in front of her. A blindfold, with convex padding for the sockets of her eyes was affixed, blotting out all light.

Carmella next felt Aboud's hand on her exposed sex. He rubbed it gently and she could feel the smoothness of a gel being applied. To her increased dismay, she felt the same applied to her rear.

Aboud had greased Carmella's holes, fore and aft. He lingered at her rear aperture, pushing his fingers deep inside. Carmella moaned and trembled in fear. Yes, this too was owned by her masters and this too they would take at their pleasure. Aboud massaged the entry point gently and then pushed a third and then a fourth finger into the hole. Having widened it sufficiently, he placed a small plug inside. Deflowering this hole was for him, her trainer. But the other hole, the one he had already violated, well, that was now claimed and possessed. That was free to all comers.

Aboud went to the small washstand in the corner of the cell and washed his hands. He grabbed his gray shorts from the floor and pulled them on. Pausing before the whimpering, kneeling slave before him, he shook his head. He had almost forgotten. Stepping back to the wall, he grabbed a leather object from the rack. It was a penis shaped gag, long and thick, modeled after his own tool. He admired it for a moment and then stepped over to the prone woman. He grabbed Carmella's chin, forcing her mouth ajar and rammed the business end of the gag home.

Carmella had no warning of the insertion of this thick,

coarse object in her mouth. As Aboud fastened the buckles of the gag's strap to the back of her head, Carmella whimpered and whined as best she could. No matter, the gag straps were affixed and that was that.

Now Aboud was finished and he walked to the cell door, recovered the keys from the hook in the wall and unlocked the door. Carmella flinched as the heavy clanging of the door signaled his exit.

CHAPTER SEVEN

Now, Carmella was alone again. But not alone in her cage, temporarily protected from abuse. No, she was chained to the stool, her legs akimbo, her naked sex available for use, her hands useless, pinned against her sides. As the silence of the cell settled around her, she explored the feelings of her confinement. The thick, hard presence in her ass was a quite new sensation. At no time had she ever let anyone fool with her back there. Her ass rape at the hotel hardly counted as she had been heavily drugged. And now her ass was plugged, exposed. At the same time, Carmella's tongue explored the massive presence in her mouth. It was long and hard and, as she felt its contour, she realized that it was in the shape of a cock.

The shock of the discovery that her mouth was stuffed and invaded by a penile facsimile, together with the invasive presence in her back side, brought home to Carmella, as it was in fact intended, that no part of her body was to be free from abuse by her masters. She remembered Aboud's words. She was property, meant only for the pleasure of others. She would be trained, broken. Well, she was broken. She would do anything to avoid pain. She would obey any and all commands, even the most scurrilous.

Carmella's sobs soon softened and died out as the numbness brought by inactivity and time enveloped her. Her reverie was broken after not too long a while by the opening of the cell door. She heard the keys dropped on the hook, the shuffle of feet, the approach of a body. Aboud had laid a pillow on the floor between Carmella's legs and she felt the heat of the person who knelt there. Hands were placed on her thighs, widening them further. A hand rubbed her sex lips, stroking them and pulling at their fulcrum below her belly. Carmella twitched as her pleasure nub was grabbed and pulled. The hand left and a soft pressure was placed against her opening. She knew what it was, the head of a cock. It rubbed softly up and down until Carmella's sex lips softened and she could feel them begin to engorge with blood. Without further ado, and assisted, no doubt, by the lubrication applied by Aboud, the cock struck home and pierced her.

No sexual frenzy for Carmella this time, just the steady pounding of a hard cock in her loins. Yes, she could feel the heat rising as she was pummeled, but not like before. She knew that this was not for her, but for the pleasure of the owner of the instrument inside her. Was it Aboud? Or was it another? How many men would she have to service? As the steady, rhythmic penetration of her sex continued, Carmella's thoughts became less about her long-term predicament and more about the rising sexual pleasure in her loins. She felt herself unwillingly pushing back against the pressure behind her. Her breasts, which dangled over the edge of the stool on which her stomach and abdomen lay, swung back and forth as her body transferred the movement of her hips.

Suddenly, she sensed the presence behind her stiffen, heard a grunt of satisfaction, and felt the warm flooding into the depths of her belly. She wasn't done, but he was. He pulled his cock from her slit and, stopping only to wipe it clean on her raised behind, rose and stepped away. The cell door clanged shut and Carmella was alone once more.

Seven more times over the next several hours the cell door opened and shut, admitting another tormentor. Or the same one, Carmella had no way of telling. She could feel the ooze of sperm that leaked from her pussy and down her thighs, the itchy stickiness as it dried. Once there had been more than one man. She could hear their banter, not understanding a word of the Arabic dialogue, but understanding its meaning clearly. Finally, she felt herself being lifted from the stool, her blindfold removed, her ankles freed. It was Aboud, her trainer. He quickly dragged her to the shower, rinsing her with the cool water, soaping her body. He ran a small hose up Carmella's slit, washing out the remnants of jism that remained.

After washing her fully, scrubbing her with a sharp bristled brush, he removed her gag, belt and bracelets. For the first time, Carmella stood before him without the accouterments of her enslavement. Aboud motioned Carmella to stand in the center of the room. As she did so, he pulled a narrow table from the far wall and motioned for her to lie on it. Carmella complied hesitatingly, for she felt sure that this was to be another round of pain and torture, a new variant on the punishments she had already received, punishments earned by her merely by her status as an unprotected female.

But it was not a punishment that was in order. The top of the table was covered by a thin mattress, making it almost comfortable to lie on. Carmella, lying face down, felt her ankles and wrists affixed to the corners of the table. Aboud ran his hand softly down her back and she trembled. Then, instead of a blow, she felt his strong hands begin to massage her back and shoulders. It was warm and rhythmic and brought Carmella a wave of relief. Her eyes welled up with tears as she let her tension release.

Aboud's hands worked their magic on her back, her neck, her thighs. He massaged her feet and arms before releasing them and rolling Carmella onto her back. He now began his massage of her front, her stomach and breasts. Carmella watched this dark skinned man as he worked purposefully, intently. His shoulder length hair draped his face. A bead of sweat rolled down his right temple. As he noticed her gaze on his face, he cooed softly to her, a strange sound that soothed her.

As her breasts were massaged, Carmella felt the warmth returning to her loins below. It was clear that Aboud's efforts had shifted from the merely relaxing and soothing to a more directed purpose. Her breasts were kneaded softly, the inside of her thighs stroked. By the time Aboud placed his hand on her sex, Carmella was already writhing in pleasure. As she felt the hand separate the lips of her pussy, she moaned softly. She watched Aboud's head drop between her legs and then felt the pull of his lips on her clitoris, a long and luxurious pull.

Carmella's eyes jammed shut as the pleasure of Aboud's oral ministrations coursed through her. She felt his tongue penetrate her, strong and long, delighting the depths of her now moist and torrid sheath. She arched her back as she felt the pleasure mounting to a crescendo within her. Her moans were now cries as her orgasm pulsed through her,

Aboud's tongue and lips driving her beyond her limits of control. After her first explosion of passion, Aboud slowed his oral stimulations, paused to let Carmella's mind drift back from semi-consciousness, and then began again.

Carmella strained at her confinements as Aboud's tonguing drove her to paroxysms of pleasure so intense it was almost pain. Twice more Carmella climbed the mountain peak and fell into oblivion.

At last Aboud raised his head, rubbing her moisture from his mouth and chin. He appreciated the panting female before him, weighing her responses, knowing that she was being drawn deeper and deeper into her dependence on him. He rubbed her sweat covered belly and breasts, now leaning over the female form and sucking gently at the twin peaks of her breasts. Grabbing her chin firmly, but not harshly, he turned Carmella's head to his and pressed his lips on hers. His tongue pushed into Carmella's mouth, filling her oral cavity with its heat. Carmella melted as she met Aboud's invasion on its own terms, running her tongue against his, sucking gently on it, wanting it, needing it.

Aboud abruptly pulled away and released Carmella's bonds. After ensuring that she had recovered enough from her ordeal of pleasure to stand, Aboud pulled her off the table and on to her feet. He dragged to the center of the room and pushed her to her knees. He left her momentarily, unlocked the wall-mounted cabinet, and returned with a straight edged razor. Carmella was still dazed but she registered the presence of the sharp instrument and shuddered with fear. Aboud grabbed her cheeks with one hand and, holding her head steady, began to scrape her scalp with the blade. Carmella could feel the sharp edge as it slid across her skull. Her own sweat served as the lubricant as the small, seedling like growth on her head was swept away. Too frightened to move, Carmella's heart ached as she recalled her beautiful, flowing locks, brown and curled, the product of years of care. She knew what this man was doing. He was shaving her skull to keep her bald, to keep her naked, as naked as she could be, to impress upon her her lowly caste: that of an animal or chattel, kept for his pleasure and the pleasure of others. He was demonstrating his mastery of her.

It was clear now. Her body was totally at the mercy of her masters. She would be used as they wished, given pleasure at their discretion and be kept abject for their purposes.

When Aboud had finished scarping her head, he folded the razor and tossed it aside. Carmella's face had been jammed into his stomach as he had shaved the back of her head and she could taste and smell his maleness, his strength. She also knew that his sex had risen and was rock hard. He proffered it to her now. She knew what was wanted, what was, in fact, demanded, and she complied.

Stroking the head of the cock gently with her lips, Carmella gently caressed with her hands the base of Aboud's sex and the heavy sack that lay beneath it. She ran her tongue across the tip of his member and then pressed her head forward, drawing it all the way in. She had done this before for Jeb and others. She knew what to do and how to give pleasure this way. She drew now on all of the knowledge, intent on showing her skill, proving herself worthy of her master's desire of her.

Aboud placed his hand on the back of Carmella's head and pushed her further down along his cock until Carmella could feel the head of the cock pressing against the back of her throat. She was, at first, surprised and anxious as she felt her breath cut off and the natural gagging reflex rise. She fought off the urge to push away, to resist her master's will. She forced herself to relax, to give in, to let the head of Aboud's cock delve past her throat's entrance and beyond. Aboud reveled in the pressure on his manhood, calculating slowly how long Carmella could resist the impulse for air. He could feel her tentative resistance and then her submission. He could hear her insistent gurgling as she struggled against the urge to wretch and vomit. He held her close, making sure that she had submitted fully, and only then withdrew, letting Carmella suck air into her lungs.

Aboud had, of course, maximum control of his own sexual powers, and he let Carmella work hard and long at her task. Holding her head with both hands, he pulled her back to feel her lips on the head of his cock, pushed her slowly into his body, to force the hardened sword of flesh back down her throat. When he felt that it was time, he let the juices begin to flow up through him. He began to pump furiously and relentlessly into her mouth. Carmella's hands tried to push him back, choking now, being battered by the thick, hot tube of meat in her mouth. When Aboud came, she could feel the warm pasty liquid splash against back of her mouth. She consumed it, compelled to suck Aboud's discharge down her throat.

Aboud slowed now, letting his cock soften in Carmella's mouth, letting all of the ejaculate drain from his cock. Satisfied that he had emptied himself, he pulled his still tumescent rod past Carmella's lips and released her. Carmella collapsed in front of him, breathing deeply, tears again flowing down her face. She hardly noticed when he stepped away again returning with her belt and bracelets. Pulling Carmella to her feet, her affixed the belt and locked her rebracleted wrists again to her sides. He pushed a bottle of water past her lips and Carmella mechanically drank the water that flowed into her mouth. She was indeed thirsty, but also wanted to drive out the taste of Aboud's manhood. When she had finished, Aboud pushed her over to her cage and motioned for her to get in. Carmella sank to her knees and edged herself over to the cage door and then slithered in, drawing her feet in behind her. The cage was shut and locked.

There was enough room for Carmella to sit crouched on her knees or to scrunch up on her side. She chose the former as she watched Aboud tidy the cell, restocking the razor and other implements of her debasement. He mixed a batch of porridge like substance and placed it in a feeder on the side of the cage. Carmella had not eaten for it seemed like days and her stomach rejoiced at the smell of the viscous glop. Fitting an upside down bottle of water to the side of the cage, Aboud stepped back and took in his captive. She was doing well. It would not take long to get this one ready, he thought. But he needed to be certain that she was fully reconciled to her servitude before she would be permitted to service the guests and customers upstairs. But it was only a matter of time.

After Aboud slammed the cell door shut, Carmella desperately gulped the food from the feeder on her cage. She was able to suck it from the tube that poked inside, a simple pressure needed to get it to flow. It had no real taste, but it was substance and she had no thought for culinary delight. When she was sated, she let herself go and cried.

So thus, Carmella was drawn deeply into her slavery. Whippings, fuckings, her mouth invaded by a score of pulsing cocks. Aboud's mastery of her was total. She lived and breathed for his presence. Only his face she saw, the rest of her tormentors and abusers leaving her blindfolded as they used her at their whim. She gladly proffered her rear opening to him when he came to demand it, and then this passage too became available to all takers. Only Aboud purposefully drove her to orgasm; his beatings of her were intermittently separated by passionate, determined sexual arousal and pleasure. It was not long before Carmella began to respond quickly and whole-heartedly to her abuse by the others. Once a cock was proffered to her lips, prodded against the opening of her ass or pressed between the lips of her pussy, she began to feel heat rising in her loins, her mind clouding with need for pleasure.

Aboud had shown her the way. She could survive only if she could learn to relish and desire her own abasement. She became obsessed with the need to be filled and accepted her beatings and torture as the necessary price to pay.

It was ten days later, although it seemed like years to Carmella, that her routine was changed as well as the circumstances of her confinement. She had graduated, the first phase of her training complete. She needed now to be readied for her service in the business areas of the brothel. She panicked when Aboud, after blindfolding her, dragged her out of the cell. She had thought of the doorway as the edge of her world, a world she had learned to cling to as a means to survival. But now she was being driven past it into unknown territory. Her whole being trembled. What new torments were to be imposed on her? Was she being shifted to a more terrible fate?

The answer came quickly as Carmella was led into a large room. She could feel carpeting under her feet, a deadening of sound in the room. In her cell, the clanging of the door, her own screams and moans in pleasure and pain, seemed to echo off of the walls. But this room was silent, almost deadly so.

Carmella was pushed to her knees and the blindfold removed. Her hands were still affixed to her sides. There were men, five large, tall men, dark as Aboud was, similar in visage and in their terrible hardness. Aboud stepped in front of Carmella and spoke.

"Today you join the community of your sisters who serve us. You are removed from your cell and your cage so that you can better perform your duties and prepare yourself to please our guests. The rule of silence is still imposed on you. While you will now be permitted to have contact with other females, slaves such as yourself, you will not speak to them. You will not touch them unless on our command. You will not touch yourself except with our allowance. You will obey all orders given to you. You will make your body available to any who desire you in any manner they choose. Do you understand this?"

Carmella was stunned by this speech. To leave the protective womb of her cell was a terrifying thought. But the opportunity to leave its crushing confines was, at the same time, a vast relief. She would not die there as she had sometimes surmised. She would be permitted to live better than the animal that she had become. She would do anything to please her masters and to become a person again. She answered Aboud timidly, her voice disused. "Y, yes, I understand." Her voice was a mere squeak.

"When you speak to a master you will address him as lord, do you understand?"

"Y,yes, lord."

"I leave you now to the pleasure of these men, your masters. When they are done with you, you will be shown your quarters and be shown how to prepare yourself on a daily basis. There will be an instructress who you will obey as if she were one of us. You will address her as madam." Aboud now stepped forward to Carmella, running his hand over her still shaved head.

"You will remain in my specific care for now and I will see you again later."

He then walked form the room, exiting the door behind Carmella. She looked up at the five men before her. She was ready to please them.

She was used well for more than three hours, every portal stuffed several times over, often more than one at a time. She was whipped, beaten and generally abused. She sucked cock after cock gladly. She was in a sexual frenzy. Finally, her tormentors tired of her and she was left alone, collapsed into a pile in the middle of the room. Shortly after they exited three women entered. One, a large boned matronly sort carried a thin, leather encased crop. The two other women were young, pretty. They wore nothing except a collar around their necks and bracelets around the wrists and ankles. Carmella took little notice of them as they lifted her to her feet and escorted her from the room. She was almost literally dragged down a short hallway and then down a flight of stairs.

Here was the dormitory for those slaves being prepared for the world upstairs. Carmella was taken to a shower and rinsed. The water partially revived her and she was able to take in her surroundings as she was being toweled down. There were two rows of beds, chains descending from the wall on each one. A kind of platform sat in the middle of the room, with some kind of padding on its top. On the far end of the room were a column and more chains. The walls were stone, like her cell had been, but the floors were carpeted in a deep red. The beds had only sheets to cover them, white and blue striped. Small pillows sat at the heads of the beds. Carmella could see the fixtures to bind ankles and wrists at the corners.

The two naked girls who assisted Carmella did so in absolute silence. The one was slightly taller than Carmella, with dark ebony skin. He features were European, with the exception of her plump, dark red lips and the beginnings of a curly black mop on her head. The other girl was slender and almost alabaster white, blond stubble on her head. They both bore whip marks, a splash of fear darting from their eyes.

The matron spoke. "You are assigned bed three. Now you will rest. Tomorrow you will begin your training. We have a few simple rules. You will remain silent except when spoken to and you will obey at all times. You will be available to the masters at all times and to such of your sisters to whom you are given. You see the platform in the center of the room? You will be required to perform there both alone and with others. You will service me as I demand."

The matron paused to ensure that her instructions had sunk in. Carmella was attentive to the point of fixation.

"You will remain clean. Your training will be comprised of learning proper deportment and how to serve as a slave. You will be shown how to display yourself and how to decorate your body to entice. You will learn to dance, how to walk, how to sit and kneel. Do you have any questions, slave?"

Carmella hesitated to speak, but gathering her courage stuttered out an almost silent, "No."

Immediately the crop descended across her breasts. Carmella yelped out in pain. As she tried to step back, the two women to her sides grabbed her arms and steadied her. Suddenly she remembered. "No, madam," she blurted out. The matron nodded, now satisfied.

"Here you have no name. You are registered by your number and will be kept track of in that fashion. You will answer only to the name 'slave'. Do you understand?"

"Yes, madam."

"Good." And to the two other slaves beside Carmella, "Place her on bed three. Confine her wrists only. Place a blindfold over her eyes so she can sleep."

The matron reached out and stroked the side of Carmella's head almost lovingly. "Do not be afraid little one. You will do fine here. Once you have been trained sufficiently, your life will improve. Do well and obey."

Carmella was led to the narrow cot, the third in the left side of the room. The two women guided her down and affixed her wrists to the top corners as they had been instructed. Carmella was blindfolded, a sheet dawn over her body. As she drifted off to a much-needed sleep, she reveled in the softness of the bed, the ability to stretch out her legs, the pleasure of a pillow.

CHAPTER EIGHT

Jeb stared into the black waters of Hymelion Bay as the launch made its way towards the yacht that lay at anchor a mile and a half offshore. It would take the launch twenty or thirty minutes to cover the distance. Jeb was glad for the time to think and brood. Tonight he was to take the first real step in finding and saving Carmella.

He had little information about what had happened after he and Carmella had separated following the fiasco at the casino. What information he did have came from the American Consular official who had been permitted to speak to Carmella briefly and one short letter from Carmella that had come out of Calipha addressed to Carmella's parents. They, of course, would not share the letter with Jeb since they felt, and rightly so, that he was responsible for the terrible predicament that their daughter was in.

The information that he had been able to pry out of the Consulate and piece together from his short conversation with Carmella's parents was that she had been arrested at their hotel three days after she was supposed to have left. She had been charged with prostitution, bribery of the police, fraud, tampering with evidence and a host of lesser crimes. But why had she still been at the hotel three days after she was supposed to leave? And where did all these phony charges come from? They were all, to say the least, out of character for Carmella. Something had happened and Jeb could not figure out what. He was stunned when he learned that she had given a 'confession' and that she had had a trumped up trial after which she was sentenced to seventeen years of servitude to the State. In Calipha, he had learned, penal servitude for women meant principally sexual exploitation of the worst kind. In effect, slavery.

When Jeb learned that Carmella had been arrested, he stayed drunk for about two weeks, berating himself, wallowing in self-pity. But then he snapped out of it, dried out, and went to work setting to try and set his wrong right.

A call on the Calipha embassy in Athens got him nowhere. There were no charges against him pending in Calipha and they would not corroborate that Carmella was a prisoner there or the status of her case. "Confidential State information," they told him. As to the money he owed, if given the opportunity, Jeb would have paid double or triple the amount. But it couldn't be done. No one would acknowledge the debt, so there was nobody to pay.

Jeb considered the possibility of hiring mercenaries to get into Calipha, find Carmella, and bring her home. But Jeb didn't have the money for that, or the contacts. What he did have was his talent for making money. Unfortunately, he had blown most of what he had at the gaming table the night Carmella had been lost. But there had to be an angle. There had to be some way of turning his expertise into a ticket into Calipha so that he could search for Carmella himself. Once he found where she was, maybe he could bust her out himself. Or make a deal for her.

As it was, the opportunity to surreptitiously enter Calipha literally came to him. He was nosing around some financial contacts when he learned that a very high placed member of the Royal Family was looking for a financial advisor to handle investments, cash flow and revenue related issues. His one non-financial asset was a friend from back home who was connected to the right people. Using this friend, he obtained false papers and a passport in the name of Paul Turner. Paul Turner was a friend of his in the financial world who had died in a car crash a couple of years before. Using his name provided the perfect resume to apply for the financial advisor position.

Armed with this false identity and curriculum vitae, Jeb, now Paul, managed to get himself an interview for the job. He sailed through the interview and before he knew it, he was winging his way to Athens for a final meeting of approval with the Prince.

And now he found himself on this small boat, making his way to the only chance he knew of to sneak into Calipha and begin his search. The bay was rough and the salty spray stung his face as he peered over the bow. Those lights ahead, the running lights of the largest yacht he had ever seen, were to Jeb lights of hope, but hope tinged with uncertainty. It had taken weeks, months, but finally a plan was in motion. Could he find Carmella? Could he save her? Where was she now?

* * * * * * *

At the moment that Jeb was being carried inexorably to his rendezvous, Carmella was undergoing training in the underground belly of the Adeem pleasure palace. She woke to her first full "day" in the training area as she had gone to sleep, chained to the head of a bed in the dormitory. She was naked, her hands locked to the corners of her bed. She had no idea how long she had slept, but it could not have been long, for she awoke groggy and confused. She was awoken by the dormitory matron, a heavy set, staid women, dark-skinned, as the natives of this Middle Eastern emirate were dark, dressed in a dull, dark brown, shirtwaist dress and black leather, low heeled shoes. Her face was broad and flabby, her eyes almost black. She carried a slender but stiff, rattan cane, encased in leather, about three feet in length.

"Up, up, up," she barked to Carmella as she poked her with the cane. "Get up slave!"

Carmella felt the sharp bite of the cane as it was jammed into her ribs.

"Get up!" the matron hollered. "Get up, wake up!"

The cane was poked even more sharply into Carmella's side.

Carmella's eyes were wide open now, as the memory of where she was rushed into her consciousness. What had seemed momentarily dreamlike was actually real. She quickly recalled her painful lesson from the day before. The matrons must be addressed properly. "Yes, madam. Yes, I am awake. Please, I'm awake."

The matron eyed Carmella for a moment. Carmella, bound as she was, could only await the matron's pleasure. Suddenly, swiftly, with a practiced hand, the matron swung the cane over her head and struck Carmella across her breasts. Then pain was exquisite. The cane was narrow enough to carry a sting as it flexed when swung over the matron's head, but sturdy enough to cause a deep thumping in Carmella's chest.

Carmella cried out in pain, "Eeeeyoow!" Her arms tensed against her confinements as she made a futile attempt to cover herself. Her legs, which were unconfined, doubled up. She twisted her torso to the side to avoid another blow to her breasts.

"When I tell you to wake up, you will wake up! Do you understand?" the matron bellowed.

"Y,yes, madam, yes!"

The matron leaned over to undo the bindings that held Carmella to the bed. After doing so, she signaled Carmella to rise. Carmella rose to her feet gingerly, steeling herself for another blow with the cane. But the matron merely motioned with her head for Carmella to come with her.

Carmella followed the matron past the other beds in the dormitory and past the circular stage that stood at its center. Not all of the beds in the dormitory were occupied. But most contained confined women, chained in place. None of them were now sleeping, for when the matron had bellowed at Carmella they had all automatically snapped awake and come to immediate attention. Many of them had experienced the cane across the breasts for waking too slowly, some more than once. It was not an experience they wished to repeat.

No daylight found its way to the training area located in the bowels of the mansion that was the House of Adeem. It was, in a very real sense, a dungeon. In it, the training routine was so varied that the young women, all chosen for their beauty and potential as compliant and dutiful sexual servants, had no basis for determining the passage of time. The rest periods and meal times were of random lengths. The training sessions were not conducted in any structured way. There was no routine for a slave to rely on to measure the days and hours of her imprisonment. In a very real sense, time stood still.

Physical abuse was both routine and arbitrary. It was not only given out as punishment for transgressions. Some beatings were administered for the pleasure of the masters, the trainers. Some were given as exemplars for the benefit of the group. Some seemed to be given just as a matter of routine, not for the pleasure it gave anyone, not for any remedial purpose, but just for the purpose of inflicting pain on the victim.

Carmella was to learn today that at the end of every rest period, one could hardly call it morning, a ritual whipping was administered. It was not a purposeless beating as was sometimes imposed. It had a purpose. Each "morning" whipping brought home to the trainee that pain awaited her. It tenderized her body, sensitized the new slave to the fact that she was in bondage, a chattel to be trained. It was a portent of the rest of the day. Moreover, it prevented any slave from falling between the cracks. It would not do for any slave in training to believe that she had beat the system, so to speak, by failing to make a noticeable error during that training period, or by managing to please all of the trainers and matrons who had charge of her throughout the day. No, every day must bring home to the slave that she was living each moment of her existence under parole. Pain and suffering were to be driven home as the norm. Freedom from pain was to be earned.

Daily beatings were all well and good, but it would not do to have the slaves emerge from their course of training scarred and broken. Therefore a delicate touch was needed. Later, when each ounce of torment inflicted by a client resulted in compensation to the House, such concerns were out of place. After all, slaves could be, and were, often replaced.

And so, Carmella was directed by the matron to a post that stood outside the door to the dormitory. It was placed strategically so that each time a slave entered the dormitory, they would remember what awaited them when they emerged. The matron signaled Carmella to stop next to the post. Although Carmella still did not know of this daily practice, she knew what a whipping post looked like. The fact that she had been stopped next to one caused her stomach to turn over.

"Raise your hands," the matron said matter of factly. Carmella complied. Her wrists were affixed to the top of the post. It was not so high to cause her to lift up on her toes. It was just high enough to make sure that her arms were clear of her body and that there would be no obstruction to the whip.

The matron was well trained, having administered hundreds of whippings. The whip was kept hooked on the side of the post, convenient, ready for use at all times. It had a thick handle and seven one inch wide strands of leather, each 24 inches long. It was designed to cause pain, but not to scar. Its effectiveness was measured by the coloration of the recipient's skin. A certain hue of red was expected to be raised, over the breasts, the front and back of the thighs, the back and the buttocks. Five strokes for each area, twenty-five strokes in all, scientifically administered.

Since this was Carmella's first experience at the daily whipping post, she was entitled to some instruction.

"Slave, attend," the matron barked. Carmella was all ears.

"Each time you emerge from the dormitory, you will submit to a whipping at this post. You will receive twenty-five strokes of the whip. You will not cringe, you will not move. You will not cry out or scream. You will suffer your experience at the post in absolute silence. Do you understand?"

"Y,yes, madam," Carmella managed to reply, her trepidation rendering her almost speechless. One would think that someone who had been beaten and tormented as much as Carmella had would have become inured to the pain. But just the opposite was the case. Because the beatings and whippings she had been administered had been so severe, had terrorized her beyond rational thought, Carmella's fear of pain had been magnified. She feared pain now more than she had ever feared it in her previous life. She did not need to rationalize this fact, she merely had to, as was intended, experience it.

Carmella readied herself for the blows. "Turn your back," the matron ordered brusquely. Carmella presented her back for punishment. The first stroke slapped across her back, the sting of the leather straps making her wince with pain. It was followed rapidly by a second, a third, a fourth and then a fifth. As each blow landed, the burning in Carmella's back intensified. Their machine like rapidity threatened to overwhelm her. There was no reason for the matron to pace the strokes. It was the fact of the beating, the sensitivity of the skin that it caused, and the discipline imposed on the sufferer that was important.

The stream of blows set Carmella's back afire. She cringed and tightened her muscles, gritted her teeth, all for the purpose of helping her stand and absorb the punishment.

The next series of blows, to her backside, were tolerable, although still painful. Matron knew the superior ability of the gluteus maximus muscles to absorb pain, so the strokes came all the harder.

It was the strokes to the back of her thighs that ultimately set Carmella in motion. After the second blow, she began a little dance. The moans that she had been suppressing became little cries. Well, matron had a fix for this. Putting the whip aside for the moment, she reached for a strap hanging on the side of the post. It took her only a moment to apply the strap to Carmella's ankles and affix them to the post.

The thighs now immobilized, the whipping recommenced. Of course, the count of five started over. Carmella knew she had sinned and that she had certainly earned a further punishment for her disobedience. She resolved to sin no more and managed to hold in her cries and moans as the statutory five strokes were administered.

She had made it through three fifths of her torment. Ten more strokes were in store. Carmella felt pity for her poor helpless breasts as she anticipated where the next strokes would fall.

The matron released the strap from her ankles and ordered "Front!"

Carmella turned her body around. She had her eyes closed, her face down, all of her muscles flexed as she anticipated the coming pain as her twin orbs were assaulted. The whip, being functionally designed, was just long enough to strike both breasts at once.

Carmella counted mentally as each blow was struck. "One..., two..., three..., four..., five". Her breasts stung, insulted by the hard application of the leather thongs of the whip, her nipples two points of fiery pain. All of her psyche was devoted to standing and taking it, to remaining silent, to obeying the command she had been given, to avoid further punishment for failure.

The next five blows were across the front of her thighs. They were painful, stinging, but Carmella tolerated them, counting down in her mind this time, as she knew that each blow of the whip was one less that she had to suffer. "Five…, four…, three…, two… and… one," she counted mentally. She had endured. She collapsed in relief, supported only by the chain that was affixed to her wrists.

Carmella's entire body was enflamed as the result of her assault. Her skin, in the areas belabored by the whip, were a dark pink, almost scarlet. The lesson had been learned; the price of life was pain.

CHAPTER NINE

Carmella was now taken to the common shower area so that she could bathe. It was a large, white tiled room with a series of showerheads along one wall. Since slaves were not permitted to touch themselves, unless under the direct command of a master or a matron, she would be washed by the slave on duty there. Carmella lingered as long as she could under the warm water. The soft pummeling of the stream of water enraptured her. It was a reminder of things past, of what she had been before.

After Carmella had completed the wetting of her body, the duty slave stepped forward to soap her. She was a thin girl, dark of skin. The hair on her head had started to come in. It was just beyond stubble, almost one half inch long. Her eyes were almost black, with thick black eyebrows above them. The girl's body gave testament to a recent beating, as angry red welts ran across the front of her thighs. Her breasts were pert, with prominent nipples, wide at the base, but tapering to a fine point.

Yesterday, or what passed for yesterday, Carmella had seen two of her fellow captives when she emerged from her marathon sexual orgy with the trainers. However, she was tired and attentive mainly to the forbidding figure of the bulky matron who was wielding a rattan cane. So this was the first time she had seen a fellow inmate up close.

The girl was naked. A small disc dangled from her nether lips that were, like Carmella's, free from hair. She wore wrist and ankle bracelets of leather and a thick leather collar around her neck that nearly dwarfed her face and shoulders. A tattoo had been etched into her skin just below the belly button. It was an ornate "A", surrounded by flourishes. Arabic writing was scrolled beneath it.

Since no speech was allowed, the black haired girl began working in silence. The matron sat on a bench opposite the open shower area, watching intently, biding her time for when a blow with her cane would be appropriate. Carmella had already earned one punishment today and she had no desire to earn another. Yet she had an almost uncontrollable urge to speak to this young woman, to compare stories of torment. Suddenly the sadness of her plight renewed itself. As the young woman soaped her body, neglecting nothing, scrubbing hard with a washcloth, Carmella's hands hung uselessly at her sides. She could not touch her own body. She could not talk. She could not linger under the warm water. What was her future here? How long would she be under the callous eyes of the matrons?

In Carmella's mind, to have women serve as the actual jailers made things immeasurably worse. Women were crueler than men, at least to other women. These bulky, almost masculine, women were sure to be resentful of the beauty and youth of their charges. It was doubtful that they would miss any opportunities to deliver suffering. And the idea that women would facilitate the reduction of other women to property, chattel, seemed to Carmella a betrayal of the worst kind. If she could not wrest sympathy from other women for her plight, where would she get it?

The matron sat staring at the spectacle of Carmella being washed. The young girl who was attending her motioned Carmella to step back under the shower to rinse off. As she did so, Carmella noted just a glint of warmth in her eyes. So there was camaraderie! This woman, who obviously had already spent some time in this mad hell, had preserved something. There was a spark there. It was possible to stay human. Carmella's eyes softened, returning the gesture of the other young girl.

Suddenly, the matron barked out a command, "Stand out!"

Carmella had no idea what that meant, but the other girl did. Reacting swiftly, she halted her attentions to Carmella and stepped towards the matron. She placed her feet apart, placed her hands behind her head. Carmella quickly followed suit.

"Getting friendly, eh girls," the matron crowed. "Having a little looky, looky?" She had stepped before the two women. The girl next to Carmella was quaking. Carmella felt a deep sinking in her stomach.

"Getting to know each other, eh? Well I think I can help you get better acquainted." The matron motioned to the dark haired girl. "I think you ought to give your new friend a present. Yes, something sweet to remember you by." She held out the cane she was carrying.

"I think you ought to give your new friend five strokes on her ass with this, that's what I think. What do you think, slave?"

The black haired girl responded with a tremulous "Y,yes madam."

"And if they're not hard enough, I'll put you down for twenty, understand."

"Y,yes madam."

Carmella's spirit was crushed. For a moment, only a moment, there seemed to be some hope. But hope was outlawed. Warmth between human beings was outlawed. She was going to suffer her second caning in an hour, her third beating of the day, all for the exchange of a glance of humanity.

The black haired girl took the cane from the matron and stood behind Carmella.

"Not a peep out of you, slave," ordered the matron. "Stand and take it. If you move, we'll start again, and this time, I'll wield the cane."

Carmella felt no need to respond. She closed her eyes and braced herself for the painful strokes. She heard the cane whistle in the air. "Crack!" The force of the blow almost pushed her off of her toes. "Crack!" The pain shot through Carmella like some creature devouring her from within. "Crack!" Now Carmella was about to scream. She believed the matron's threat. If these hurt so, what would five from her be like? She held herself in with all of her might. "Crack!" The pain shot through her again. Only one more to go. "Crack!" Carmella let a mild whine escape. She grimaced; she was lost!

The matron let out a snarling laugh. "Almost made it slave. But I said not a peep. Now you're really going to get it. Stand against the wall!"

Carmella started to wail, low, deep in her throat. She jumped to the wall and pressed herself against the cold, white tiles.

"This time you can wail and scream all you like," the

matron said. "Enjoy yourself."

If the fives strokes from her fellow slave were hell, these five were from the last circle of hell. Carmella wailed and screamed at that top of her lungs as each crushing blow found its mark. One after the other, the blows struck home on Carmella's already raw ass. Each one sent a message of searing pain. She could barely stand, as the blows seemed to literally suck the energy right out of her body. As the blows came in rapid succession, Carmella's plaintive, piteous voice echoed through the room.

Although it seemed like an eternity to Carmella, the caning was over quickly. She remained pressed up hard against the wall, sobbing and moaning, her whole being overwhelmed with pain and despair.

"Get down on the floor, slave! Face down!" the matron commanded.

Carmella moved instantly, despite the distracting pain and the wreckage of her small glimpse of hope. She laid herself prostrate on the tile floor, still sobbing and moaning.

"Hands at your sides, slave!" the matron barked.

Carmella complied.

"Now, you see what you've done. You've gotten your backside all marked up. It's really red, you know. It'll be black and blue before long. And everyone who sees you will know that you've been a naughty girl."

The matron circled Carmella, eyeing her handiwork. "All this for a little peaky boo. I hope it was worth it. And you have this little creature to thank for it, don't you?" She motioned to the black haired girl who had resumed a position of attention, hands behind her head, legs spread.

"Now I want you to thank her."

Carmella could barely hear the taunts through her sobbing. It took a moment to register that she had been given a command. "Yes, madam," she blurted out through her tears.

"Say, 'Thank you, slave'."

"Thank you, slave," Carmella managed to whimper.

"Good. And now, I want to give you something that will help you remember this little party we've been having," the matron said.

As she spoke, she stepped one leg over Carmella. Crouching down over Carmella's head, she raised her dress with two hands, exposing her sex. Suddenly a thick stream of foul smelling urine coursed over the back of Carmella's head. It ran down the sides of her face, down her back, onto the floor. The matron had unleashed a torrent of hot, yellow piss, as if she had been saving it up for the right moment.

To be pissed on was a totally new experience for Carmella and one she had never accounted for even when she had projected the torments and tortures that she might be forced to suffer as a slave. It had never occurred to her that someone could get joy from showering another with their liquid wastes. If she thought that she had reached the nadir of all possible humiliation, she had been wrong. This was a new low, a new degradation. What others would follow?

Finally, the stream slowed to a trickle, then drops, and then stopped. Still holding her skirt up at her waist, the matron addressed the black eyed attendant, "Come over here and lick me clean, slut."

The matron stepped over to the wall and the girl jumped to obey. The matron sat on the bench and spread her legs.

The black haired girl knelt before her and pressed her face between her thighs.

"Lick it good, slut!" the matron commanded.

The black haired girl lapped at the fleshy gash before her. She absorbed the remnants of the woman's discharge and, since she had not been ordered to stop, continued to tongue the matron's hairy gash.

"Oh, yes, slut. Yes, yes, yes. Keep going, kiss my clit, suck on it."

The matron spread her legs wider and pressed her hands on the back of the young girl's head. She kept moaning in pleasure as the experienced tongue and lips between her legs drove her passion. A deep moan escaped her lips, her eyes rolled back. Suddenly, she clamped her thighs about the kneeling slave's head and pushed the mouth servicing her cunt harder, deeper into her musty center.

"Oh, oh, oh," the matron yelled as she began to come. Still holding her cane, she whacked it down against the slave's ass and yelled, "Yes, yes, suck it, suck it!"

Finally, her crisis passed. She released the head of the black haired slave and pushed her away.

"A good job, slut. Make sure you leave my juices on your face for the rest of the day. In fact, you're such a good cunt licker that I think I'll tell some of the girl's to come pay you a visit. Would you like that, slut?"

"Yes, madam," the girl answered in a small voice, not much more than a whisper.

The matron stood up and stretched. "Ah, that was nice," she said, reflecting on the dutiful attention that the black haired slave had given her.

Carmella had calmed down by now, although the crushed feeling remained in her breast. She lay where she had been left, in a puddle of piss, its sharp odor all around her. She felt as filthy and degraded as she had never felt before in her life. It was beyond imagination. What more could they do to her? What more would they do to her? "Survive," the little voice inside her said, "survive."

The matron was right. Carmella would never forget this day. She bemoaned her imprisonment in a world where she could never again give recognition to a ray of humanity from anyone. How quickly a moment's peace had turned into hell! Her survival was everything. She was desperate to avoid the humiliation and pain she had suffered here. She would do anything to avoid it.

"Get up, slave," the matron ordered. And to the black haired girl, "Wash her again. And be snappy about it."

Resentment welled up in Carmella towards the black eyed girl, the girl who had foolishly sinned against the masters, against the rules. She had led Carmella down a path of pain and abasement. She cringed at the thought of this girl touching her again. "Some day, some day, I just hope that I can repay this one. I'll make her suffer," she thought.

Carmella's skin crawled as the black haired girl washed her body again. This time the shower stung as it ran down her raw backside. The towel was agony as the girl patted her rear end softly. Carmella could hear her sniffling, ashamed and forlorn at what she had caused, at what the matron had made her do.

"You can cry," Carmella thought. "I'm the one who was beaten."

The matron reaffixed the black haired girl to the chain on the wall where she had been restrained when they had come into the shower area. She motioned Carmella to follow.

The feeding area was next, and even here Carmella was to face debasement and humiliation. The feeding area was a small room with benches running along the sides of a square table. Three slaves were eating when Carmella and the matron entered. There was another matron in the room. Carmella's tormentor left. Carmella moved to take a seat at the table when she was halted by the outstretched cane held by the refectory matron. "No you don't," she said. "You have to earn the right to sit at this table, slave. Get on your knees."

Carmella obeyed without question, but wondered what could be in store for her next. She was answered almost immediately.

The matron took a bowl from the table and filled it with the oatmeal-like mush that was contained in the larger, common bowl. She brought it to the corner of the room and put it on the floor. "Crawl over here," she ordered.

On her hands and knees, Carmella crept to the corner. The message to her was clear. Not only was she a slave, she was the lowest of the low, not fit to eat with the other slaves. She fought back tears as she moved towards the bowl.

"Hands behind your head!" the matron shouted. Carmella complied. "Now, eat. And eat it all!"

In spite of her morning of abuse, or maybe because of it, Carmella was ravenously hungry. She bent her torso as low as she could and began to lick the mushy substance from the bowl. As she consumed the gloppy mass, the room stood silent except for the scraping of spoons and the clicking of her bowl as it rattled against the floor and wall. The food, whatever it was, tasted like a combination of chalk and mud. But to Carmella it was delicious, a sensuous experience. For the moment, she was able to filter out her surroundings, suppress the thoughts of where she was and what was being done to her. The food represented a sensation other than pain. And so, no matter how awful it was, it was good.

CHAPTER TEN

As the launch pulled closer to the large yacht, Jeb pulled out of his reverie and began to mentally prepare himself for his meeting with the Prince. He looked around the launch at its other occupants. Aside from the two man crew, there were two rough, black haired, dark men, dressed in western attire. One was young and tall, broad shouldered, a bushy mustache across his upper lip. The other was older, smaller of build and wiry. A scar crossed his right cheek. Between them sat two women wearing long, grey burkhas. Only the tips of stylish high-heeled shoes peeked out from under the bottom hems. Jeb had seen them as they got out of a large black limousine near the dock. The women had been escorted by the two sinister men. They seemed to stumble their way to the launch as if they were wearing high-heeled shoes for the first time, taking tiny, shaky steps. The men had to hold their arms to keep them from falling to the ground.

The dock itself was an out of the way place, clear across the peninsula from Athens. Why the Prince had anchored his yacht in such a far away and isolated place was a mystery to Jeb. Why would he make what appeared to be his family and their bodyguards get off here to visit Athens, assuming that's where they had come from? It was at least a two hour ride along the coast. There was nothing at all between here and there. And this was just a small fishing village, tiny white houses made from limestone and plaster, fishing boats with nets strewn across them, a tavern. During his research into the Prince and the quaint customs of the natives of Calipha, Jeb had become aware of the Prince's penchant for privacy. If Calipha was a nation that tolerated slavery, there were probably slaves right there on that boat. That might explain the use of this remote port facility and the anchoring of the yacht more than a mile offshore.

Jeb had to fight back a feeling of revulsion at these two Arab women. Living in the dark ages, socially speaking, but so ready to avail themselves of the benefits and accoutrements of Western styles and technology. How could they justify living with a man who was really nothing more than a slaver and a whoremaster? Didn't they realize that by living their lavish lifestyle, by accepting the social compact that allowed their men to own other women as slaves, that they were as morally bankrupt and ethically guilty as the men?

Jeb stared at the two women with contempt. Then he remembered. If they were relatives of the Prince, he better not make enemies of them. He was undoubtedly going to have to eat a lot of dirt before he was through. He couldn't afford to have the Prince, or anyone else, think that he had any qualms about the job, that he gave a fuck how these oil rich nomads practiced their medieval customs on the women of other lands. And so he smiled politely, nodded to them. "Go fuck yourselves," he thought.

The engine was noisy, and the wind whipped away

words as they were spoken, but he thought he heard one of the women say something. He could not see their mouths behind the cloth that covered their heads and their entire bodies. He could barely make out eyes behind the gauze-like windows over the upper parts of their faces. One of the men leaned over and said something to the woman who had apparently spoken. Jeb could not hear the words, but he figured that the woman was being reprimanded for speaking to a stranger, and a Westerner at that. The woman stiffened and nodded to the man.

Now they were within feet of the large ship and the launch cut its engine and drifted in to the side of the yacht. There were stairs that ran down from the deck and Jeb stood and motioned for the two women to precede him. The security guys waved him off. "You go first," the one said, smiling.

They were probably worried that he would look up their dresses as the walked ahead of him on the stairs, Jeb thought. But then he remembered about the high heels they were wearing. Undoubtedly they had to take them off to walk the stairs and didn't want to reveal their ankles to this infidel. Oh well, he would go with the program.

As he reached the top of the stairs, he was met by a thin, officious looking man, dressed in a suit, but clearly an Arab. Jeb assumed that the man was the Prince's major domo. He was.

"Ah, Mr. Turner. I am so glad you made it. You had a good flight, a nice journey?"

"It was fine," Jeb replied.

"My name is Rashid; I am the Prince's servant. You're room is waiting for you below decks. I'll have one of the sailors show it to you. The Prince will be engaged this evening. He will see you in the morning, after you have rested."

"Thanks," Jeb replied. "It's been a long day." The major domo waived to a hovering sailor. He picked up the bag that had been brought up on deck by one of the launch hands and motioned for Jeb to follow him. The burkha-clad women had just reached the deck, apparently with much assistance from their bodyguards. Jeb turned towards the bow, and smiled and waived as he walked to the stairs to his cabin below decks.

Once Jeb had walked away, the major domo motioned to the two men to escort the women toward the stern. The women were led down the length of the ship to an above decks cabin. The cabin was a sumptuous reception room, decorated in the theme of a Bedouin chief's tent. The walls were hung with fabrics, resplendent with Arabic designs, red and black. Covering the deck was a plush, soft oriental rug of the finest weave. There were large pillows strewn on the floor in a semi circle facing a larger leather covered armchair. The armchair was low, almost as low as the pillows on the floor, as if its legs had been cut, which, in fact, they had. This enabled the Prince to sit almost at the level of his guests, but just a little higher as befitted his rank and dignity. There was a large, semi-circular table in the form of a crescent that sat between the pillows and the chairs, something to place sweet meats, dates and other delicacies on for the guests.

The two men and two women entered the cabin by a side entrance. The men motioned to the women to kneel on the floor. They sat on the pillows. After they were settled, they waited silently.

It was only about ten minutes later that there was a

commotion outside a door at the front of the cabin. Without further ado, the Prince arrived, preceded by a security guard. The Prince was tall, with stylish grey hair. He appeared fiftyish. He was fit, his strength showing through the loose, white polo shirt that he wore. His slacks were tan and he wore thick, leather sandals on his feet. He had sparkling blue eyes. He strode across the room his arms open, a smile on his face.

"Demetrius, I am happy to see you," the Prince exclaimed. The two men had risen to their feet. The smaller man moved forward, his hands extended, the other stood between the two women, his hands on their shoulders.

"My Prince, it is always a pleasure to see you. Especially under such auspicious circumstances," the one called Demetrius answered. The men exchanged a hug.

"Oh, yes, yes, yes," the Prince replied. "A fortuitous rendezvous." He motioned to the door and two male attendants entered carrying tea, teacups and a small bowl of fruit. After depositing their burdens on the table, they moved to opposite walls and stood at attention. The security guard positioned himself at the side of the room and assumed an observant stance.

The Prince motioned his guests back down to their seats. "Please, have some tea with me before we discuss business. I know your Western ways, but they bore me. I am a man of the desert. Time is to be savored, not spent like some cheap currency."

"Of course, your Highness, of course."

The Prince bowed to the other man in the room. "You're assistant, I presume?" the Prince inquired.

"Yes. Please forgive my rudeness. This is Paolo. He got

the whole thing rolling really. If it wasn't for him we wouldn't even be here."

"Well, hats off to you Paolo. And I do like the merchandise. Thank you for the emails. The pictures were delightful. I confess, before we even start, I'm sold. I am at your mercy."

The men laughed, all knowing that the Prince was known as a hard bargainer, a hard man. He would pay a fair price, but no one would walk away thinking they had got the better of him.

The men sat, drinking their tea, exchanging pleasantries. The women remained kneeling and silent. After about fifteen minutes, the Prince said, "Well, then, let's see what we've got."

"At your pleasure, your Highness," Demetrius replied, "at your pleasure."

He and Paolo stood up. The two women were still kneeling in between them. "Where should we start, vanilla or chocolate?" he asked the Prince.

"Oh, vanilla, please. It's my favorite," the Prince replied.

Paolo pulled one of the women from her knees to her feet. She stood shakily. The two men reached down and grabbed the hem of the burkha and lifted it up. As it rose, the Prince could see a pair of pale feet stuffed into blood red, high heel shoes. A small chain connected the ankles, gleaming in the light that shined down from the small overhead chandelier. Demetrius and Paolo took their time in raising the burkha. First, a set of graceful shins, then well-toned, youthful thighs. Slightly higher, and the Prince could see the apex of the woman's legs. A white bikini bottom shielded the woman's sex, but the beginning of a flat, taut stomach could be seen. A belt passed around the woman's waist holding two small wrists in place at the well rounded hips.

The men paused. "Do you like what you see so far, your Highness?" Demetrius asked, sure of the response.

"Oh, yes. Very nice. But you are killing me with apprehension. More, more!" the Prince replied.

All three men chuckled. The curtain began to rise again, up, over the stomach, revealing two firm globes of flesh restrained by a white bikini bra. The bra was about as small as it could be while still remaining legal. The breasts burst out on all sides, held in only by tiny triangles of white. Two hard buttons of flesh were poking the inside of the fabric, nipples that were hardened by fear. The woman was shaking visibly. Her hands were opening and closing in frustration at her hips. Who she was, and where she had come from had yet to be revealed. But already the Prince could see that she was a prime female specimen. If only the face justified the body.

Without further fanfare, the two men pulled the burkha free. The first thing the Prince noticed were the pair of bright blue eyes, eyes that were widened in fear, the pupils darting from right to left. Then he took in the delicate nose, the full, fleshy lips distended by a gag which pushed the woman's cheeks out and extended her lips, revealing strait, white teeth. The hair was honey gold, and fell down below the shoulders, strait and full. The neck and shoulders were like porcelain.

"Demetrius, Demetrius, you have justified my faith in you," the Prince exclaimed. "And the pictures, oh, they do not do this creature justice." He rose to his feet and walked quickly around the table. He stood in front of the woman whose eyes were now focused on him. He took her all in, appraising her with the eye of an expert.

"May I," he asked as he reached out to touch her flesh.

"Of course my Prince, be my guest."

The Prince reached out his hands and placed them on the woman's hips, just below the belt. He ran them down the outsides of her thighs, down to her knees and to her calves. Then, bringing himself to his full height, he placed his hands on either side of the woman's head and peered into her eyes. The eyes peered back, staring into their doom.

"Let's see the rest of her, shall we?" the Prince asked, breaking his gaze from the girl's.

"By all means," Demetrius replied. He reached for the back of the bikini top and pulled free the small knot that held its two ends together. The top sprung free and fell to the floor at the woman's feet. The two breasts fell, causing them to sway, the flesh to ripple slightly. The nipples were hard, the skin pulled tight around the pale, small aureoles. The breasts were full and firm, large for this delicate a frame.

"Ah, a joy to behold," the Prince cooed. "What things of beauty." He reached for the twin orbs and stroked them gently. The girl stiffened, but did not move as Demetrius and Paolo held her firmly by her arms, pulling them together behind her back to better accentuate the delights in front.

"Oh, I must see the rest!" the Prince entreated. "Let me see her cunt."

Demetrius pulled a small penknife from his pocket and clicked it open. Deftly he slit the right side of the bikini bottom and then the left. Placing his foot between the woman's ankles, he forced her legs apart to the length of the chain that bound them and, unceremoniously, pulled the bikini bottom free from the back.

The prize was revealed. The pubic hair had been trimmed precisely to fit within the small piece of fabric that had hidden it tantalizingly away. It was honey colored, like the hair above, thin, more like a wisp than a bush. For the first time, the girl moaned. Her knees weakened and the two men had to hold her up to prevent her from falling. The eyes now were shut, clamped tight as if to keep out the reality of what was happening.

The Prince leaned over and pushed aside the thighs. He ran his right hand along the lips of the woman's sex, probing gently. The lips were thick, engorged. The entrance was dry, but with a slight manipulation of the bud at the top, began to glisten with the woman's secretions. After a few moments, he was able to slip a finger between the lips and feel the soft, gentle flesh inside.

"Please, your Highness, you must see the ass!" exclaimed Demetrius. "You will swoon."

The Prince nodded affirmatively and the girl was spun around. Confronting the Prince were two half moons of pale flesh, even paler where the sun was not allowed.

"Ah, paradise," the Prince rhapsodized. He placed his hands on the two cheeks and pulled them apart to reveal the small star-like entrance to the woman's bowels.

"I believe that you are looking at virgin territory, your Highness," said Demetrius.

"By my beard, I believe that you are right," the Prince replied.

He fingered the entrance gently. The woman stirred, pulling at the arms that held her in place. Paolo pinched a nipple firmly.

"Be still, cunt," he ordered.

The woman cringed in pain and ceased to struggle.

"You have delighted my heart Demetrius," the Prince exclaimed "but I must see the chocolate. Please, let me see her."

"Of course," replied Demetrius. He spat a few words in Greek to Paolo who, in turn, whispered something into the blond girl's ear. She fell to her knees.

During this exhibition, the other woman had remained stock still, kneeling before the low table in front of the cushions. She now rose swiftly, drove her shoulder into Paolo and made for the doorway. Paolo stumbled backwards as the woman, although hobbled, was able to dash past him.

There was nowhere to go. Outside the door were only the deck and the sea. But perhaps the young lady lurking under the grey burkha preferred drowning to the shame and humiliation that loomed before her. Perhaps she had no other thought than a last protest against the cruel men who had captured her and were about to strip her nude and present her as a piece of merchandise to be appraised and, presumably, purchased by this man they referred to as the Prince.

She did not get far. It was a simple matter of Demetrius sticking out a foot and the woman went sprawling. She landed on the rug with a loud "thump", as she had no hands with which to brake her fall. Even then she tried to squirm away. Paolo, recovered by now, grabbed at her leg and pulled her back to the table. Grabbing the other leg, he lifted her into the air and then unceremoniously dropped her to the floor.

Stunned this time, the still shrouded woman lay

motionless. The men all laughed.

"A spirited one, eh?" remarked the Prince.

"All too spirited I am afraid," replied Demetrius.

"Oh, in my experience there is no such thing as too spirited," the Prince commented. "The more spirit, the more satisfying the victory."

"Well, I bow to your expertise, your Highness. After all, you are the connoisseur," Demetrius replied.

"Then let's unwrap this piece of chocolate," quipped the Prince as the two other men dragged her to her feet.

Sparing the strip tease, the men swept the burkha off of the young woman, revealing an ebony colored, black haired beauty. She was fleshier than the blond, wide hips, a prominent rear end. She was wearing a black bikini, the top straining to contain two large breasts, the bottom clinging tightly to the mound between her legs. Demetrius quickly stripped the small pieces of cloth away and presented the tall, shapely, caramel colored women to her prospective owner.

Unlike the blond woman, this woman's eyes were alight with fire. The two men struggled to restrain her as she twisted and turned her body in rebellion against her captivity. Her breasts dodged back and forth as the two Greeks manhandled her body. The Prince stood back and watched, amused.

"Let's string her up in the frame," the Prince suggested.

"Anything to calm this bitch down," Demetrius answered.

The men dragged the struggling woman to a rectangular shaped structure at the rear of the cabin. It stood on a broad base of wood, set off from the wall by several feet. There were circlets of steel at each corner.

The woman's protesting voice could be heard from behind the gag. She dug her now shoeless feet into the carpet to inhibit her progress to the frame. It was to no avail as the two men who held her were experienced with subduing recalcitrant women and her ability to resist was frustrated by the confinement of her hands to her waist and the chain which restricted the movement of her feet.

While Demetrius held one arm in check, Paolo freed the other from the belt at the woman's waist. Not without some strain, he lifted the arm into the air and fastened the wrist into the circlet at the right upper corner of the frame. When that was done, he reversed roles with Demetrius and the woman's left wrist was affixed to the upper left corner.

The woman was now dangling from the frame, which stood about one foot taller than the length of her body with arms extended. Tying off her feet would be the tricky part since her legs were so much stronger than her arms. But Paolo had the remedy for that. Before undoing the chain that confined her ankles, he gave the woman a vicious jab to her solar plexus. Her moan could be heard through the gag. She was immobilized with pain, her breath taken away. Taking advantage, Demetrius and Paolo undid the ankle chain and fastened the woman's ankles to the right and left corners of the frame. She now hung in the frame, her arms and legs splayed, her naked body fully distended and, finally, at rest.

While the two Greeks were struggling with the black woman, the Prince's bodyguard had taken hold of the blonde by her hair. He held it firmly, discouraging any rambunctiousness on her part. She remained kneeling, meekly, as surprised as any of the others at the black woman's outburst.

The guard handed the blonde off to Paolo as the Prince advanced towards the now well displayed, coffee colored body. The woman recommenced her struggle, straining at her bonds, refusing to concede her captivity. At the same time, able only to breathe through her nose, she was wheezing loudly, trying to catch her breath. To the Prince, this was a most gratifying spectacle. As the woman gyrated in place, her breasts were tossed to and fro, shimmering and glancing off of each other. Her breath was labored, in a gross simulation of passion. Her straining at her bonds accentuated the fine lines of her muscled legs and arms. This was a woman in fine trim, well exercised, toned.

The three men stood and watched the woman with admiration. Finally, the Prince decided that enough was enough. He stepped to a cabinet in the wall and drew out a three foot long wand. He glanced at Demetrius who nodded his approval. Placing the wand at the entrance to the woman's sex, the Prince pushed a button on the wand's side.

"Crack!" The wand produced an explosive charge in the woman's vagina. The electric pulse passed through her entire body, stiffening her. A moan escaped her gag. The Prince placed the wand again against her slit. Frantically, the woman shook her head, pleading against another demonstration of the wand's power. Smiling, the Prince pushed the button once more.

"Crack!" The wand exploded again. This time the sound that emanated from the woman was more like a high pitched whine as her whole body tensed momentarily and then relaxed. As the wand was placed in position a third time, the woman began to sob. The Prince looked into her eyes and spoke to her. "No more trouble, yes?"

The woman nodded, desperate to avoid a further example of the pain that can be administered by a determined and ruthless man. The Prince handed the wand to an attendant who put it back into the cabinet.

"Now, let's see what we have here," he said to himself. Approaching the helpless, shapely, young woman, the Prince ran his hands along the insides of her thighs. The Prince's skin was not strictly white, but more mauve. It blended nicely with the woman's coffee colored covering. He moved his hands to her breasts, massaging them, assessing their fullness. The woman's hair was black, neatly trimmed around her sex, cut short and curly on her head. She had an aquiline nose, almost Roman, and her lips were broad and dark. Sweat poured off of her as she tried to regain her breath. Her brown eyes followed the Prince's movements as he rubbed her waist and stomach, stroked the prominent lips below. He walked behind the frame and took in her firm and ample rear, letting his fingers trace the valley between her cheeks, poking at the puckered orifice at their center.

"Gentlemen, I toast your very delightful merchandise," the Prince addressed the two Greeks. "Now, let's get down to business."

Returning to their seats at the table, the men began to haggle. Demetrius, knowing that he would never get it, wanted $150,000 for the pair. The Prince, knowing that it would not be accepted offered $30,000 for the black girl. "As you know, my dear Demetrius, white women, even ones as delectable as this, are a glut on the market right now. I have a dozen white women waiting for masters. The black one I like because she has spirit and will it give me sport to tame her. I think $30,000 is generous."

"My Prince, please stroke the thighs of this blond woman. If there are a dozen women as lovely as this in your whole country, I would give you this one for free. As to the black one, why, I must confess that I turned down an offer for her for $100,000, and all because I knew that you are appreciative of fine flesh. In all good conscious I could not part with them for less than $145,000."

The dickering went on for some time. At the urging of Demetrius, the Prince took the blond woman on his lap and stroked her sex. It was not long before she commenced to whimper; her face became flush, the skin on her breasts, taut. Demetrius unlocked her legs so that they could be spread wider. The value of the black woman was discussed back and forth. At one point the Prince rose from his seat to reexamine her assets. He took a nipple in his mouth, the woman now complaisant. She shivered as he bit down.

Finally, the price was agreed upon. More tea was served.

"Tell me Demetrius, I have never seen gags quite like these. There are no straps to hold them in place. What prevents them from being spit out?" the Prince inquired.

"I am happy that you asked me this," Demetrius replied. "They are of my own design. Let me show you."

The Greek took a small key from his pocket and addressed it to the center of the gag in the white woman's mouth. As he turned it, her cheeks deflated, her mouth relaxed. With a gentle tug, he pulled it out.

"I got the idea from a book about a woman who is captured and bound and gagged for transport. You see the outer portion of the gag consists of a bag of a viscous gel. The interior is a spherical spring. When the gag is placed in the mouth, you turn the key and the spring expands. The bag, being flexible and gelatinous, spreads out to fill the voids in the woman's mouth. When it expands to fill the whole mouth, it is now too large to be extracted without turning the key back. I have found it most effective."

"May I try it?" the Prince inquired.

"Certainly. Be my guest."

The Prince took the gag and proffered it to the white woman's mouth. She had been silent as the gag was discussed, too horrified at her circumstances to speak. But at the prospect of the gag being reinserted into her mouth, she came alive.

"Please, oh please, don't do this. Please don't do this to me. Please let me go. I won't tell anyone. I'll do anything you want, just please let me go." Her voice was plaintive and weak.

The Prince laughed. He looked at the girl. "Well, it has a voice. And just what would you do if I agreed to let you go?"

Encouraged, the blond girl replied, "I'll do anything you want. I'll, I'll sleep with you. I'll fuck you. I'll fuck all of you. I can do it, I'll be good. I can suck your pricks."

Tears were rolling down the cheeks of the young girl. She was on the edge of panic. She had heard her selling price being bandied about and hardly believed what her ears were telling her. She was desperate. As desperate as anyone could be.

"But, little one, you will do that anyway," the Prince replied. "I own you now and I can do anything I want to you." As he said this, he stroked her hair, patting her head, as one would do with a child. The woman's voice broke as she protested against this dreadful message.

"But you can't do that! It's wrong! Please, please, I don't want to be owned. You can't own me!" She started sobbing now in earnest, twisting and turning her confined wrists, trying to pull herself from the Prince's lap.

But the Prince had her firmly in his grip. He placed his hand around her throat and pushed his thumb up against the center, stifling the girl's voice. "Now, be a good girl and open your mouth," he said in an almost soothing tone, a voice practiced at the art of manipulation, a voice used to being obeyed.

Her eyes full of tears, the young, blond girl meekly opened her mouth. The Prince inserted the gag and began to turn the key. Quickly, the girl's mouth was filled with the gelled bag. She whined softly as her lips began to spread and the gag pushed her jaws apart. When the key met hard resistance, the Prince pulled it out. The girl's mouth was distended as it had been before, her eyes shut, her brow wrinkled in dismay.

"If you would like," the Greek said, "I could easily supply you with a few hundred of these. You can see the benefit of not having to deal with straps and the like. The girl is silenced and yet you can see her whole face."

"Yes, yes," the Prince replied, "I will have my man talk to you. Perhaps I can license these in my own country. There is a huge market, as you know."

"My idea exactly, my Prince. I will await a call from your servants."

"By the way, you haven't told me how you came to possess these two delectable sluts," the Prince remarked.

"As I said," the smaller Greek replied, "it was all Paolo's doing. Perhaps he should tell the story?"

The Prince nodded and attended to Paolo.

"Well, you see," he started in his gruff, low voice, "my aunt runs a small hotel near my village. It is an out of the way place, frequented mostly by honeymoon couples and adulterers. These foreign sluts showed up two days ago. They got off of the bus and walked right in, demanding a room. A single room, they said, with one double bed.

"My aunt let them have the room and then spit on the ground. She knew that these two were lovers. She called me. She wanted their money, of course, but she also wanted them out of the hotel before they committed any of their fouls acts on each other. So I arranged a pool party, at Demetrius' house. I got my aunt to invite them, to show them some Greek hospitality. She introduced me as her nephew and told them I would drive them. She said they would meet wonderful, interesting people, an artist, a poet, something like that."

Paolo paused to take a sip of tea.

"So I brought them there and, well, there was no party, of course. Demetrius and I quickly subdued them and stashed them away in the cellar. From there we contacted you."

The Prince laughed. "Two lesbians who thought they could walk into a respectable Greek hotel and practice their shameful arts on one another. Well, they'll get their chance now. What about their things, didn't they let anyone know where they were?"

"Oh, no," Paolo replied. They made out postcards and asked my aunt to mail them, but of course, they did not get mailed. Their cell phones were in their handbags at the hotel. No calls for two days. These whores have just vanished off the face of the earth. All of their belongings were destroyed, except their cash, of course. I had to give that to my aunt."

"And vanish they will, my good boy, vanish they will,"

said the Prince, laughing.

"And now, your Highness, we will take our leave. I have enjoyed your hospitality," said Demetrius as the two Greek men began to rise.

The blonde girl had been kneeling at the Prince's feet while her betrayal and capture was being described. She had remained motionless, despair and fear freezing her in place. But now that the Greeks were leaving, she came back to life. She knew that the last connection with her former life was about to walk out of the room, that with the Greek men gone, she would be left with the Prince and whatever cruel fate he had in store for her. He was obviously a fiend, a demon. He had mentioned slaves; he had tortured her friend and lover.

The woman tried to rise, a desperate sound in her throat. But her hopeless attempt to gain mercy and compassion from the men who had captured her was short lived. The Prince placed his hand in her wheat colored hair and jerked her head back. She collapsed to the floor. The Prince called out to Demetrius.

"Wait, you haven't told me their names."

"Oh, yes," Demetrius replied. "The blond, she's British, her name is Vicki. The colored girl, she's from Jamaica. Her name is Yolanda. Enjoy them!"

After the men had left, the Prince snapped his fingers and pointed to the cabinet that held the wand he had used on the brown skinned girl. An attendant quickly produced it.

The Prince dragged the blonde by her hair to the middle of the room and threw her to the floor. "Kneel," he commanded. The girl rose to her knees, trembling.

"I am going to remove your gag and loosen your wrists.

If you make a single sound or make a single move you will taste this." As he spoke, he poked the wand into the girl's chest. The girl responded with an emphatic nod of her head.

The Prince removed the gag and loosened the confinement to her wrists, unfastening the belt from her waist. "Put your hands behind your head, elbows up," the Prince ordered. The girl complied.

"Straighten up, spread your legs."

She did as she was told. The Prince now turned to the stretched and dangling Jamaican. He poked her stomach with the wand. "Do I need to give you another taste?" he asked her.

She too had heard the discussions between the men. She had caught the callousness with which they had talked about her body, its use. And she had felt the kiss of the electric wand. She shook her head violently.

The Prince motioned to the two attendants who jumped to lower the girl from the frame. In a moment she was kneeling by her lover's side, hands behind her head, her fine breasts jutting out.

The Prince addressed the two women. "Now one of you is going to suck my cock and the other is going to receive a lashing. Which will it be?" He circled the women, pushing and prodding with the wand. He lifted the darker woman's breast with its end; he rubbed its length along the white woman's slit.

The naked, trembling women were following him with their eyes as he walked about them. They were sure that he was serious and that one of them would soon be writhing in pain, receiving the business end of a whip.

"How to decide?" the Prince mused. He placed the

wand under the chin of the woman once called Vicki and pushed it up, causing the woman's head to distend backwards, forcing her to look into his steely blue eyes. "Your lover has already felt pain tonight. Maybe it should be your turn."

The blonde struggled to hold back her tears as her body shook in fear.

The Prince turned to the other. "But you have been very bad tonight," he teased as he pushed her head back. "Maybe you should be punished."

There was no longer fire in the coffee colored girl's eyes, just terror at the prophecy of pain that she could not have imagined she would ever suffer. To be whipped!

"I know," the Prince continued, "we'll do it fairly." He took a coin from his pocket. "Heads, you suffer the lash," he said pointing to Vicki. "Tails, and its you," he said, referring to Yolanda.

He tossed the coin into the air. Both of the frightened women followed its descent. It landed almost silently on the rug. Heads.

Vicki started to blubber and whine. She was overcome by her desperate plight. She could only imagine the excruciating pain of being beaten with a whip. She started to pee.

An attendant deftly retrieved a bowl he took from a shelf and shoved it under her. Her liquid quickly filled it.

"Now you've wet my nice rug," the Prince said menacingly. "I will have to punish you for that."

Vicki quailed in fear.

"But later, maybe tomorrow," the Prince added. "Tonight is just for fun."

He motioned to the attendants who scrambled to grab

the young woman's arms. She lost control of herself and started to beg and plead.

"Oh God! No! No! This can't be happening! Please don't whip me, please!"

The attendants were remorseless as they dragged her to the center of the room. The Prince pushed a button on the wall and a chain descended. Two bracelets dangled from its end.

Vicki continued to beg and plead as her wrists were placed in the bracelets. When she was affixed, the Prince pushed another button, which caused the chain to rise. Vicki was lifted until her feet could no longer touch the ground. She twisted and turned frantically. One of the attendants brought over a belt. He wrapped it around Vicki's ankles and bound her legs together.

The girl's body glistened with sweat caused by her terror. The Prince stood before her, admiring her gleaming white skin. He grabbed her torso and put his mouth to her right breast, sucking at the distended nipple. He rubbed his hands up and down her thin but shapely body, as if preparing the skin for the torment to come.

Standing back, he signaled to the bodyguard. The bodyguard smiled. This was one of the perks of his job: the torture of helpless women.

Turning to the kneeling Yolanda, the Prince spoke to her, tapping her cheek with the wand. "Now, my sweet, I know that sucking cocks is not your sex act of choice, but if you fail to pleasure me adequately, you will take your turn on the chain. Do you understand?"

The girl nodded quickly, eager to avoid her lover's fate. The Prince walked to his chair and removed his throbbing, erect member from his pants. He sat down and motioned the kneeling woman over.

Yolanda, fearful of earning the Prince's wrath, remained on her knees and shuffled her way over to where the Prince sat. She kept her hands behind her head. She too was crying.

"When you bring me off, the whipping of your lover will cease. So her fate will be in your mouth along with my cock," the Prince instructed her. "And if you so much as nick my cock with your teeth, I will pull them all out myself, one by one."

The Prince placed his hand on the woman's head and drew her to his loins. At the same time he signaled the bodyguard who had produced a four-foot long lash. As the black haired Jamaican circled the Prince's cock with her lips, the guard delivered the first stroke.

The whip snapped loudly as it scoured the dangling woman's flesh. Her wailing now became a scream as the fire of the lash's tip burned into her. The first blow struck her proffered buttocks; the second, the back of her thighs. The guard took his time, carefully coiling the whip before delivering the next blow. He circled the suffering woman and delivered a crackling blow to her left breast.

"Oh! Oh! Oh!" the young girl cried. Another lash struck her right breast. A dark red bruise emerged at the point of contact. The fabric on the walls, the thick rug, deadened the woman's laments.

In the meantime, Yolanda was working assiduously on the Prince's cock. Frantically, she tongued the head of his prick, slid her thick, dark lips down its length. Her hands were still behind her head as she bobbed up and down, her lips tight, her tongue swirling furiously. Desperately, she worked to end her lover's torment.

Leaning back, his eyes pinned to the spectacle of the white woman's torture, the Prince luxuriated in the workings of the black woman's mouth. An experienced cocksman, he knew how to prolong the moment of crises. He could control the release of his seed. He would not do so until his enjoyment of Vicki's suffering was sated.

Vicki had just felt her twentieth stroke of the lash when, the Prince's desire for the pleasure of release outweighed his delight at Vicki's screams. He allowed the mouth that encircled his manhood to drive his passion to its limit. Feeling his impending release, Yolanda accelerated her exertions. As he came, he flooded Yolanda's mouth with his discharge, drops of sperm drooling from the corners of her mouth. The Prince signaled his climax by a loud groan, grabbing the head that was delighting his rock hard flesh and pressing it down, finding the entrance to Yolanda's throat.

As the last diminishing throbs of his prick sent signals of pleasure to his brain, he signaled to the guard to stop. One last "crack" resounded as the guard delivered a blow to the crux of Vicki's thighs.

Vicki continued to moan and cry even though her whipping had ceased. The Prince allowed Yolanda to drink in every last drop of his discharge. When he felt his hardness start to recede, he pulled Yolanda's head from his lap. He spoke to the attendants, "Take these whores below. Attend to the blond one's wounds. I don't want any scarring." And to the bodyguard he said, "Tell the Captain that as soon as the launch has returned he's to weigh anchor and head for the open sea."

CHAPTER ELEVEN

Jeb's cabin was lusher then he expected. He had foreseen a closet sized room with a cot-like bed, a miniature sink, perhaps, and a loo down the hall. What he got was much different. The sailor opened the door to the cabin and Jeb beheld a wide double bed set amidst sumptuous surroundings, a plush red carpet, a mahogany bed stand and dresser and, about 150 square feet of space.

The sailor placed Jeb's suitcase on the stand at the end of the bed and proceeded to the bathroom where he turned on the light. The room was a full bathroom, containing a large scalloped shaped sink, an appropriately sized toilet and a wonderful glassed in shower. The tile was a pale blue background interrupted with a swirl of white and sea green tiles reminiscent of raging surf. The appointments were plated gold.

Jeb stood mesmerized. The reality of the vast wealth of his prospective employer washed over him like the wave depicted on the bathroom walls. And Jeb knew that with wealth came power. He had read up on the Prince, and read between the lines where appropriate. He knew that the Prince was a force to be reckoned with and that his charade carried great risk. But seeing these casually elegant surroundings relegated to what was essentially a low level, potential employee, made Jeb appreciate for the first time the unfamiliar waters in which he was about to swim.

His musings were interrupted by a knock on the cabin door. He moved to the door and opened it. It was Rashid, the major domo.

"Are these accommodations to your satisfaction Mr. Turner," he asked.

"Very much so," Jeb replied.

"Can I get you a drink perhaps?"

"When will I be meeting with the Prince tomorrow?" he asked.

"I am afraid that the Prince is very often a late riser. I have scheduled your audience with him for 10 o'clock tomorrow morning, if that is satisfactory with you."

"Then a drink would be greatly appreciated, please," Jeb said. "Scotch, no ice."

"It will be done," said Ali.

Five minutes later Jeb heard another faint knock on his door. He had been getting ready to take a shower and had undressed to his skivvies. An elegant terry cloth robe was one of the perks of the room and so he donned it before answering the door.

When he opened it, instead of the deferential sailor he expected he was surprised to see a small, dark haired woman holding a tray on which sat a glass and a bottle of 24 year old single malt scotch, seal unbroken.

"If it pleases you sir, I have brought your refreshment," the diminutive young girl said. Her hair was shoulder length and strait. She had a round face with delicate features. But what was most remarkable about the young lady was the fact that she was naked. Well, almost naked, if you counted the long sash-like, red and black cord that ran around her waist and down her right thigh. Her breasts were firm, plump half shells with pointed tips. Her hips were wide, her legs sultry. On her lower belly, just above her loins, was an ornate tattoo, red and blue, of a large, stylized, capital "A" surrounded by a flourish of thin, flowery lines. Jeb was glad he had put on the robe, because his cock rose to attention immediately.

"P,put it over there," he stammered, pointing to the dresser.

The young girl moved gracefully over to the dresser and laid her burden down.

"May I pour you a glass, sir?" she entreated.

"Oh, eh, of course," Jeb replied, still overcome by the spectacle before him.

The girl carefully broke the seal of the bottle and poured Jeb four fingers of Scotch. She grabbed the glass with both hands and, turning towards Jeb, bowing, head down, proffered it to him.

Jeb was sweating now. He cursed himself for being so flustered before this unselfconsciously naked woman. The ineluctable paradigm expressed itself to him: the Prince was a slaver, this woman was naked and subservient, therefore, this woman was a slave.

"May I prepare the gentleman's shower?" the girl asked in a soft, honey toned voice.

"Why, eh, yes, please," Jeb replied. Jeb felt like he was on his first date with the parson's daughter and she had just put her hand on his cock. He took a deep gulp of the scotch.

The patter of the shower water provided some relief to cover Jeb's lack of preparation for the experience of meeting with his first, actual slave. He had known that if the Prince employed him, a thing he desperately wished, he would ultimately have to confront the horrid reality of slavery. But he was not prepared to confront it so soon and not in such a tempting manner. He could not take his eyes off of the gently swaying breasts, the curvaceous hips, the prominent, hairless lips between the woman's thighs.

He called her a woman in his thoughts but she looked more like a girl. She had a freshness and innocence about her that was inconsistent with Jeb's mental image of a sex slave. She couldn't have been more than 19 years old, yet she emanated the graceful sexuality of a courtesan well beyond her years. She was geisha like in her movements and in her obvious deference to his desires.

"Sir, the shower is ready," the girl announced.

Jeb nodded, threw back the balance of the scotch in his glass and stepped towards the shower. He knew it was ridiculous, but he was embarrassed by his state of arousal. He knew he could not disrobe without revealing the evidence of his excited state to the woman. But then, what difference did that make? One more set of rampant cock and balls were surely nothing to this obviously experienced woman. He would just jump in the shower and...."

Jeb threw off the robe and quickly drew down his white boxer's to his ankles. As he stepped out of them, his manhood stood proud and erect. He pretended to ignore it and stepped into the shower. The young woman, who had removed her sash, stepped in with him.

The water made the young beauty's brown skin shiny. Jeb was taken aback by her entrance in to the shower, but admired the sheen on her skin, the way that the water ran down her body. The shower was big enough for the both of them, but not so big that their bodies did not rub up together.

"Will the gentleman make his head wet and stoop down so that I may wash his hair?" the girl asked deferentially. She stood about 5'4", coming up to the center of Jeb's chest. He would have to crouch down on his haunches for her to be able to reach his head. As he did so, the girl reached for a bottle of shampoo on a shelf and poured a quantity into her hands. Jeb's hair was wet and she had no trouble bringing the shampoo up to a creamy lather on his head.

Her hands were strong, and her fingers pressed firmly into Jeb's scalp. Slowly, with practiced skill, the girl massaged his head. Waves of relaxation passed through Jeb as he let himself be lulled by the woman's sensuous touch. He could feel her breasts nestling against the back of his head as she drew him in. Her naked thighs pressed against his back. The warm water calmed his body. The effect on him was trance like. It was more sensual than sexual. He was conscious of the beautiful body behind him, but his mind was slowly drifting somewhere else.

Gently, the woman drew his head back so that the pulsing water of the shower could rinse the soap from his hair. The girl then applied a cream rinse and Jeb felt himself drifting away again as the expert fingers pressed and rubbed along his scalp. She tipped his head back and washed the cream rinse from his hair.

She spoke now, very softly, as if loath to disturb his reverie, "Please rise, sir, so I may clean your body."

Jeb bestirred himself slowly, rising to his full height. His erection had subsided somewhat as a result of the dreamlike sensations of the massages to his scalp. But when the girl slid in front of him, her breasts dragging across his chest, her thighs rubbing up against his, he returned to a state of full sexual excitement.

Jeb had remained chaste in the months that had passed since he had last seen Carmella. Sex had been the last thing on his mind, although his subconscious dreams mixed memories of his torrid lovemaking with Carmella with imaginary scenes of her debasement. On the mornings following those nights, he cursed himself as the evidence of his involuntary nocturnal delight was on his thighs and sheets.

So when this woman rubbed her body up against his, he felt electrified with lust. As she began to soap his body, his cock stiffened to a point of high tension. She first addressed his chest. Using a soft, fibrous sponge, she spread the soap slowly and deliberately. Jeb stood helpless, his hands at his sides, as she brought her attentions lower. She rubbed the sponge against his stomach and then, avoiding his groin, dragged the sponge slowly down the outside of his thighs.

"The gentleman will please spread his legs," the girl whispered. Jeb complied, entranced by this female's sensuous attention. She ran the sponge slowly over the inside of his thighs and down his calves. As she did, she brushed her cheek slightly on his cock, sending Jeb a charge of pleasure.

The mixture of sensations, the tingling of the sponge as it ran across his skin, the nearness of the woman's body as it brushed against him, the warmth of the water as it poured over him, sent Jeb into a realm of pleasure he had never experienced. His mind was blank, overwhelmed by delectable sensations.

The sensations were heightened geometrically as the woman, abandoning the sponge, began to rub her soapy hands over his lower belly, the underside of his sex, and then the sex itself. Jeb felt the throbbing in his cock increase, his passion welling up. The girl seemed to sense this. She paused, waiting for the drive to crises to subside. After a moment, she slowly resumed her ministrations. She fondled the sack beneath Jeb's cock, and took the very tip of his manhood in her mouth. Softly, gently, she sucked on the tense, firm prick. Jeb swooned as the warmth of the girl's mouth overrode all other sensations, all other thoughts. He raised his hands, supporting his body by pressing against the sides of the shower stall. The gentle tugging on the head of his cock sent a tingling to his mind that enthralled him.

Gracefully, the young woman withdrew her mouth from Jeb's penis and slid around him so that her front was now pressed against his back. Taking the sponge up again, the woman drew it across Jeb's shoulders and down his spine. As she rubbed his sides, his focus on his cock and the need to reach orgasm subsided. Again his mind drifted to the sensuousness of the warmth of the water, the gentle roughness of the sponge as it sensitized the skin on his back and ribs. The girl dragged the sponge across his buttocks and down the back of his legs. She had now touched virtually every inch of his body. His whole body seemed alive, awake.

Having finished with Jeb's legs, the dark skinned girl abandoned the sponge once again. She rose slowly from a crouch, running her hands along the front of Jeb's thighs, her breasts against his back. As she reached her full height, she pressed her body into Jeb's. He could feel the hard tips of her breasts drag along his skin. He felt her warm thighs press against his. She placed her mouth on his back and drew it along his spine. As her left hand pressed against his stomach, her right hand found his stiff manhood.

Her touch was light, just enough to reignite the tingling that coursed through Jeb's body. Slowly, gently, she began to massage the rock hard member. Jeb intuitively knew that the purpose of the woman's expert fondling of his cock was no longer just to arouse and titillate, but that the road to his climax had begun. The hand gripped his cock firmly and rubbed the skin up and down.

The repeated stroke across the tender margin between the shaft of his cock and the head brought Jeb wave after wave of pleasure. As she manipulated his manhood, the girl rubbed her soft, curvaceous body against Jeb's back. Jeb's blood began to rise. The girl firmly grasped his scrotum with her other hand and sucked intently on Jeb's back. The rhythm of her strokes increased and she timed the rubbing of her body against Jeb's to match the intensity. Jeb could feel his climax coming. He began to moan, his thighs began to shake, his hips now thrusting to match the rhythm of the hand that encircled him. Finally, he could hold back no more, as the hand forced him over the threshold and his cock began to pulse and pump his fluid out of its tip. Wave after wave of pleasure passed through his body. He felt the young woman pull his body back into hers, maximizing the contact between their skin.

Finally, the pulsing subsided. The girl's practiced hand, sensing the ebb of his passion slowed accordingly. The grip on his balls slowly abated. His breathing, which had become intense, became languid. The girl gently, but firmly hugged his body into hers. All that was left was the gentle, warm pulse of the water as it poured itself over Jeb's tingling body.

The girl insisted on drying Jeb's body and accomplished her task with the same delicacy and skill with which she had stroked his manhood. Jeb was in a daze. He had not imagined that his first encounter with a slave girl would be like this. There was no hint in this girl of oppression, of being cowed and forced to demean herself. All that emanated from her was her dedication to his pleasure.

The girl coaxed him politely to his bed. She excused herself, with his permission, of course, and returned to the bathroom to dry herself. He was half asleep when she returned. The girl put out the light and crawled into bed with Jeb.

Her hand drifted across his lower abdomen. At the same time she pressed her breasts against him. Her legs intertwined with his. Jeb's blood began to stir anew.

He reached an arm across his body and pulled the slight girl on top of him. She stretched her body out to its full length and ran her hand along his arms. Her legs pushed at his, splaying them. Moving only her hips, she rubbed the crease of her sex along the length of his cock. He could feel the hot moistness of her cunt.

The woman began to kiss Jeb's chest. She sucked at the nipples one by one, as she drew her hands across his shoulders and down his sides. Jeb could feel a tingling in his body at this unexpected caress from the girl's lips. Her mouth then descended down his chest, kissing and sucking at his skin. Her hands rubbed at hips and then his thighs. As she reached Jeb's stomach, as her intentions became clear, Jeb moaned in anticipation.

Her hands stroked the inside of Jeb's thighs as her

mouth found his now hardened cock and drew it in. The moist warmth sent a jolt of pleasure through Jeb. Her tongue curled around the head of his solid rod as her mouth sucked it gently. She ran her tongue across the hole at the tip and then descended down his cock's length, taking it all in, letting the head pass into her throat. Jeb's entire cock was in her mouth and the heat and pressure was exquisite, almost to the point of pain. Jeb let out a loud moan and placed his hands on the girl's head.

For twenty minutes, the girl continued to pleasure Jeb's manhood. Three times she took Jeb to the edge of orgasm, each time pulling back, making Jeb wait a little bit longer. Jeb's consciousness was all but absorbed in the flow of pleasure through his body. He recognized, in a corner of his mind, the purpose of the hand job in the shower. No way could he have withheld his climax this long if she had not prepared him by taking some of the edge off of his passion.

Finally, Jeb felt he could take no more. His need to come was blinding, excruciating. His hands closed on the head that was pleasuring him and forced it down onto his cock. Into the girl's throat he plunged, her lips now circling the base of his steely hard prick. Her tongue swirled around the shaft, her lungs pulled as she poised to draw Jeb's essence. With a loud groan, Jeb came, spurting his load of sperm into the girl's throat. As he came, she furiously increased her endeavors, her hands cupping his balls. Jeb's back arched as he tried to push further into the girl's accommodating mouth. She withdrew her head, took a deep breath, and descended once more down the shaft. Jeb's cock continued to pulse as the pent up passion poured from him. Then, gradually, the throbbing began to fade;

Jeb's frenzy began to subside.

The man lay almost comatose. The slave girl gently swirled her lips and tongue over the now diminishing tube of flesh, pulling out every last drop of Jeb's cum. When she was sure he was finished, she stretched her body out next to his and nestled in the crux of his shoulder, her hand across his chest. Within moments, Jeb was asleep.

Sensing Jeb's slumber, the girl carefully arose. She drew the covering up over Jeb's body and crept to the foot of the bed. Quietly, she knelt down, her legs spread, her hands behind her back. She waited.

Jeb slept deeply that night, the intensity of the pleasure he had endured had exhausted him. The rocking of the boat and the drone of its engines acted as a soporific. He dreamt of Carmella. They were together, on the shore of a peaceful lake. She was laughing. They had both shed their clothes and he could see her breasts sway as she moved towards him. He watched as her mouth covered his prick, like she had done on the last day they had been together. Slowly, Jeb realized that he was awake. There was a mouth on his cock. He was rampant and a head was bobbing slowly up and down over his loins. He looked and saw a head with blond hair and white skin on the curved back of the woman kneeling between his legs.

He sat up suddenly, pulling his cock from the mouth that had been servicing him.

"What the fuck," he stammered. "Who the fuck are you?"

A pale face rose from between his legs, framed by long, platinum blond hair. Two dark blue eyes stared out at him.

"I am called Dina, sir, if it pleases you," the thin, young woman replied. "My master sent me to awaken you."

"Your master? You mean the Prince?"

"The Prince's servant speaks for the Prince. His Lordship, Rashid, instructed that I should be sent."

While she was speaking, the girl kept one hand encircled around Jeb's cock, gently, but firmly stroking it.

"Am I not pleasing to the gentleman?" she asked, a note of trepidation in her voice.

"No, I mean, yes, you are pleasing," Jeb replied.

Her face was smooth and her skin pale. Her delicate breasts were rocking gently as she leaned over him. He could see the gracious roundness of her hips, the ample, pale mounds of her ass. She smiled politely at Jeb's answer. Slowly, she crept forward, placing her thighs outside of Jeb's. He watched her, appreciating her beauty, his need rising. As she leaned over to kiss his chest, she eased his cock into her moist, hot canal. Slowly, she enveloped him, the clenched muscles inside her sex squeezing his penis firmly.

With practiced motion, she began to ride Jeb's cock. Jeb lay back down. His eyes fluttered as he absorbed the pleasurable strokes. He ran his hands over the girl's well-muscled thighs and grabbed the firm globes of her ass and pulled her down onto him. The girl's hot sleeve was caressing him as she moved her hips up and down. Jeb responded by bucking his hips. He moved his hands from her buttocks to her breasts, massaging them, pulling on the nipples. He pulled her torso down and took a nipple in his mouth. The girl moaned as he sucked hard on one teat and then the other. Her breath was coming fast, small cries of passion escaping from her throat. Jeb felt his climax coming and he pulled her down onto him, thrusting his hips hard into her. As he came, he could feel the girl shudder, her passion engaged, her hips pressing back at each of Jeb's strokes. As Jeb came, so did the girl, Jeb groaning and grunting, the girl emitting gasps and cries.

When their passion was spent, the girl gently drew her body off of his. His hand absently stroked her thigh and hip as he slowly recovered his senses. Suddenly, he realized that the ship was in motion. Panicking, he leapt to his feet and stared out of the porthole. There was no land! He realized that he was now a virtual prisoner on the Prince's boat.

He had expected an interview, a return to land and, hopefully, a summons to Calipha. He was not prepared to commit himself to his enterprise without an opportunity to carefully plan his next move. His mind raced. Well, he would have to deal with the cards that had been given him now. He turned to the girl. "Where are we headed?"

She was kneeling on the bed, her hands behind her, her head bent. "I do not know, sir," she replied.

Of course she didn't, she was a slave. The girl spoke softly to Jeb, "If it pleases the gentleman, I will make ready your shower now."

Jeb laughed nervously, anxious to hide his shock and surprise. "No, I think I'll take this shower alone, thanks."

The pale, thin girl slid off of the bed and knelt on the rug. She spread her legs and placed her hands at her back.

"What happened to the girl who was here last night?" he asked."

"I do not know, sir," the girl replied.

Jeb stared at her for a few moments. The girl was beautiful and certainly experienced at giving pleasure. She looked about twenty or twenty-one. She had a slight accent to her English. She sounded German, or maybe Dutch.

She was a slave. Someone had taken her and had forced her to submit to the bonds of slavery. At some time, a year ago, two, maybe even a few months ago as far as he knew, this girl had been free, living her life, just as Carmella had been. She probably had a boyfriend, a job, maybe the beginnings of a career. And he had fucked her without hesitation, without a thought of remorse. The girl evidenced no shame, no humiliation, no hesitancy at servicing him. She had even experienced pleasure. Was this what Carmella was becoming?

CHAPTER TWELVE

This was, in fact, what Carmella was becoming.

After being forced to eat her meager gruel on her knees like an animal, she was taken to a small, dimly lit room where she was fitted with her leather bracelets and collar. She was then frog marched back to the common room, her arms locked behind her. She was dragged over to a small frame and forced to kneel down before it. The matron roughly forced her to lean back on it and fastened her collar to the top. Her ankles were fastened to its sides, her legs spread wide. A ring gag was pressed into her mouth.

And thus she was left for the remainder of her "day". For most of the time, she knelt, exposed and bound, watching the comings and goings of the slaves, trainers and matrons as they went about their business. Several times trainers stopped to examine her, to feel the heft of her breasts, the tautness of her belly, the softness of her lower lips. Twice, a matron had stopped to administer several sharp strokes to her breasts, not hard enough to bruise, but hard enough to make Carmella wince with pain. And three times, trainers had stopped to use her mouth.

The first one was one that Carmella had seen before, one of the ones who had fucked her repeatedly the day she had been liberated from her cell. He had been walking by and had almost passed her when he caught her out of the corner of his eye. The man was tall and broad shouldered and as he stood appreciating Carmella's helpless state, he loomed over her. Carmella quaked with fear. "Ah, Aboud's bitch," he said, not to Carmella, but to himself. He stepped up and stroked her bald head, now rough with a day's growth. The fastening to her collar left Carmella little room to move her head, her neck was forced forwards, her mouth at the level of the man's loins. Her back was arched slightly forwards, tilting at just the right angle for use.

The man then lowered himself into a crouch and caressed Carmella between her thighs. He rubbed her clitoris gently and then stroked his finger the length of the now lubricating divide between her labia. Carmella welcomed the incipient pleasure that rose from her loins. She could see the trainer's cock beneath his shorts harden.

Suddenly, the man squeezed the lips of Carmella's pussy tightly. Instantly, what had began as pleasure turned into pain. He squeezed harder, forcing a moan from Carmella as she shifted her weight and struggled in her bonds. The squeezing continued until Carmella's eyes began to water and her moans turned into a whine. All the time that he was tormenting Carmella's pussy, he stared into her eyes, watching for the effect of his abuse. When he was satisfied, he rose and pulled his now steel hard cock from his shorts. Stepping up to Carmella, he rubbed it over her cheeks, across her lips, poking it into her eyes. Carmella's mouth remained wide and stretched, drool running down her chin, waiting for the man to ram his rod into her throat. Then, having delighted sufficiently in Carmella's humiliation, he pushed his cock between her lips and into her mouth.

The trainer took his time, repeatedly running his cock back and forth in Carmella's mouth, before finally, pushing it all the way in, past the entrance to Carmella's throat. Carmella's throat had been well used by Aboud and others during her confinement in her cell. She had learned how to relax her throat muscles, to suppress her reflex to gag. But she did not know how to breathe with her windpipe obstructed and so, as the man kept his hard, round flesh at the back of her throat, Carmella began to struggle for air.

Looking down at Carmella, the man smiled, enjoying her torment. Her body tensed and her face began to turn red. A choking sound emanated from her throat vibrating against the head of the penis that restricted her breath. The man's eyes closed, his head back, as he reveled in the pleasure that her constricted throat brought him. Just as Carmella's head began to swim, as the man felt her jaw slacken, he withdrew. Through her gag, Carmella choked and coughed, desperately pulling fresh air into her lungs.

Three times, the trainer took Carmella to the edge of unconsciousness. Each time, Carmella felt as if her life was about to end, her mind screaming, "No, no, no," her hands clenching and unclenching, straining at their confinement, her toes curled in desperation.

After the third time, the trainer looked down at Carmella's beseeching eyes, the tears flowing down her cheeks, and laughed, "Had enough cunt?" He began pumping his cock back and forth into Carmella's mouth in earnest. Its tip rammed against the back of her throat. Frantically, Carmella tried to run her tongue over it, hoping to accelerate the man's passion. But the cock merely forced her tongue aside as it pushed back and forth through her mouth. The man sought the opening of her throat as the fulcrum of his endeavors, rubbing the head of his penis back and forth across it. Finally, as he emitted a low, guttural groan, his cock began to pulse. As it did, he pulled it from Carmella's mouth and holding it in his hand, pumped it, discharging his come onto her face. The copious fluid ran down from her forehead, into her eyes and down her cheeks. The man stepped back, replacing his tool into his shorts, smiled, and walked away.

Twice more that day, Carmella suffered a similar torment. Each time, she choked and gagged as the men reveled to the feel of their cocks down her throat. Finally, after several hours, she was released, brought back to the dormitory and allowed to rest. Confined to her bed, the cum of three men dried upon her face, her chest and breasts, she cried.

For three days, Carmella's routine did not vary. A shower, some dismal slop fed to her on the floor of the refectory, and then on her knees, her mouth jammed open, ready to receive the pleasure of her masters. On the fourth "day", she was taken to one of the training rooms. There she was beaten unmercifully and left to hang at the end of a chain for four hours.

The next day, back on her knees. Then the torture room again. On her seventh day, she was taken to another training room. There she was mounted on a pole, running up from the floor, the end, rounded, pressed into her sex, forcing her to stand on her toes to avoid the pole pressing against her cervix. She was left there, standing in the darkened room, gagged, her arms bound behind her, for three hours, although she had no way of measuring the time. By the time she was released, the cramps in her feet had become excruciating, her sex sore and raw. The following day, a new torture of confinement, as she was placed in a sound proofed box, and left there for several hours, her ass filled with a thick dildo, her mouth stuffed with a leather penis.

Each "day", of course, began with the ritual beating, the ritual shower and feeding. Her treatment varied, but not its nature. Day after day, she suffered some form of confinement, violent abuse or ritual defilement. The sleep intervals were varied in length but rarely lasted more than a few hours. Maximum disorientation was the goal of her ordeal. A tired, hungry, naked slave became more malleable when she could not predict what torments she would suffer, or how long they would last.

As the days progressed, Carmella yearned for the relative rationality of her solitary cell. There she was aware of the purpose of her torments: to make her open herself sexually to the demands of her masters, to surrender her will. Now, she began to believe again, as she had during her initial days in her cell, when she was beaten continually, without explanation, without the benefit of a single spoken word, that the purpose of her treatment was to torture her until she died. She told herself time and time again that she must survive, that she must endure. But that voice in her began to fade. She began to despair of living, of ever feeling a warm touch, or hearing a gentle voice again. She began to believe that she would fade away to nothing in this terrible dungeon.

On the tenth day, the tenth real day, that is, more than twenty of Carmella's training "days", Carmella was brought to a luxurious room, full of pillows and light. She had allowed herself to be dragged there, listlessly, not caring what torture she would suffer, defeated, her mind almost blank. Her hands bound behind her, she was pushed to her knees in the middle of the room by the burly matron who had taken her there. Her neck was attached to a pole that rose from the floor. Her legs were chained to the iron rings behind her. Her head was held fixed, her body stretched to its maximum height. The matron left, extinguishing the light.

She was alone in the room for about a half hour when she heard the door to the room open behind her. She flinched as the door shut and the lights were turned on. She felt the approach of a person, his soft steps on the carpet. Then out of the corner of her eye, she saw him, Aboud! He was naked. Her heart had yearned for him during the past days, remembering only that he had allowed her respite from her suffering, had allowed her to serve him, had allowed her pleasure. Now, she wanted to call out to him, to beg him, "Please, please let me serve you. Let me have a purpose, let me live!"

But she remained silent, as Aboud had trained her to do. She watched him circle her, taking her in with his eyes, measuring her. She took in his muscled flesh, yearning for his touch. He came to a stop before her. She waited for him to speak or to act, her eyes imploring him for relief, begging an end to her suffering.

Aboud stood and watched his former charge. He could see the toll that her torments were taking on her. He could see the spark of hope in her eyes. Her body was shaking, trembling. He measured her, taking in the frail, defeated, but still desirable woman before him. Yes, she was ready.

"Slave," he spoke, "are you prepared to serve your masters?"

Carmella was startled. She was being asked to speak.

Her mind, having been benumbed by her enforced silence, searched for words. A few moments passed, Aboud piercing her with his gaze. Carmella dug down and found the words to speak, her voice frail, cracking.

"Y,yes master."

"With your mind and your body?"

"Y,yes master."

"To exist only to please those who will use you?"

Carmella was sobbing, grateful for the opportunity to beg. "Yes, oh, yes master. Please let me serve. Oh, please, please."

Aboud paused for several seconds, as if in thought. Carmella was in torment. She was not able to speak without permission, but the need to beg and plead was welling up inside her.

Wordlessly, Aboud freed Carmella's feet from the rings and released her head from the pole. He unfastened her wrists. "Please me," was all he said.

Carmella's first thought was to fall on her master's cock, to press her body into his, to feel his warmth, his strength. But she knew that would not please her master. Her master did not want her to serve her needs, but his. He was entitled to pleasure, not her. Checking herself, Carmella slowly crawled to her master's feet. She kissed them lightly and caressed them with her hands. Slowly, she ran her lips up his legs, her hands following behind them. Gently she nuzzled her head against his thighs, brushed her breasts against his knees.

Looking up adoringly at the man who had first mastered her, Carmella's mouth found his tumescent sex. Softly, she encompassed it, allowing the warmth of her mouth to be transferred to him. As she felt his prick rise, she let her tongue gently stroke the tip. She pressed her lips down on its shaft. Only one thought filled her mind, to deliver the maximum pleasure she could create to her master. He had allowed her to serve him and she would, with all of her mind and body.

For ten minutes, Carmella continued to worship at Aboud's manhood. She took his balls into her mouth while she stroked the hard flesh above. She swirled her tongue around the head that adorned it. She swallowed it whole, letting it fill her throat. As she felt Aboud's breathing increase, his muscles tense, she redoubled her efforts, knowing that very soon she would gratefully receive his discharge into her mouth. He grabbed the back of her head and pushed her down on his cock. As the steely flesh began to throb in her mouth and the salty fluid jetted down her throat, Carmella felt that she was saved. She had shown her worth, her devotion. For the first time in many days, she felt joy.

Aboud stepped back from the slave appreciatively. He had known that she would train well. He was satisfied. He fixed Carmella's neck back to the pole, leaving her ankles and her arms free. He stepped from the room and turned off of the light.

For the next three hours, a parade of men, coarse, rough men, demanding men, used to the services of slaves, came and went from the room. Each used Carmella in their own way, stuffing her moist crevasse with their hot meat, pushing past the taut ring between her buttocks and into her bowels, using her mouth. Carmella eagerly and joyfully pleasured each one of them, spreading her legs willingly at their command, kneeling down, her ass in the air, offering a choice of portals for their pleasure. Her lust for the feeling of being used mounted as the time went on. She shuddered violently each time that she received their discharge. Her sex stayed wet and ready, eagerly anticipating her next use. She lost count of the men and her own orgasms as she welcomed the hot flesh that pierced her.

All thoughts of who she had been and what had been done to her had fled. She was a slave now, she knew that, and her only joy in life, from here on out, would be in service to a master intent on his pleasure.

Concluded in Book Two

CPSIA information can be obtained at www.ICGtesting.com
Printed in the USA
LVOW04s1756110813

347337LV00001B/36/P